# Kristy's Big Day

**Look for these and other books
in the Baby-sitters Club series:**

# Kristy's Big Day

## Ann M. Martin

AN
**APPLE**
PAPERBACK

SCHOLASTIC INC.
New York Toronto London Auckland Sydney

ISBN 0-590-43899-9

12 11 10 9 8 7 6 5 4 3 2 1                                9/8 0 1 2 3/9

Printed in the U.S.A.                                                    28

# CHAPTER 1

"Old Ben Brewer was crazy. As crazy as anything. He ate fried dandelions, and after he turned fifty, he never left his house . . . except to go out in the yard to get dandelions. When he died, his ghost stayed behind. I'm telling you, he haunts our attic."

Karen Brewer looked at me with wide eyes. "Honest, Kristy. *He haunts our attic*," she repeated. Karen loves to talk about witches and ghosts. She thinks her next-door neighbor, old Mrs. Porter, is a witch named Morbidda Destiny.

Karen's four-year-old brother Andrew turned to me with eyes as round as an owl's. He didn't say a word.

"I think you're scaring your brother," I told Karen.

"No, she's not," whispered Andrew.

I leaned over to him. "Are you sure?" I whispered back.

"No." I could barely hear him.

"I think that's enough talk about ghosts," I said.

"Okay," replied Karen. Her tone of voice implied that it was foolish of me not to arm myself with information about old Ben. "But when you move into our house, you'll wish you knew more about my great-grandfather. Especially if you get a bedroom on *the third floor*." Karen made "the third floor" sound like Frankenstein's castle.

I couldn't help giving a little shiver. Why was I letting a six-year-old get away with this?

Karen looked at me knowingly.

Karen and Andrew are the children of Watson Brewer, who is engaged to my mother, the divorced Elizabeth Thomas. This means that when they get married, Karen and Andrew will become my little stepsister and stepbrother. It also means that my brothers and I will be moving out of our house on Bradford Court, where we grew up, and into Watson's house.

There are pros and cons to this situation. The pros are that Watson is rich. In fact, he's a millionaire. And his house isn't just a house, it's a mansion. Charlie and Sam, my older brothers, who have shared a room for years, will each have his own bedroom at Watson's. They could probably each have a suite of rooms if they asked nicely. And David Michael, my little brother (he just turned seven), will finally have a room bigger than a closet.

I don't benefit at all where bedrooms are concerned, since I already have my own and I think the size is fine. The main drawback to moving to Watson's is that he lives across town. I have never lived anywhere but right here on Bradford Court. All my friends are here. Mary Anne Spier lives next door, Claudia Kishi lives across the street, and Stacey McGill and Dawn Schafer live nearby. The five of us make up the Baby-sitters Club (I'm the president), and it won't be nearly as easy to run the club when I live clear on the other side of Stoneybrook, Connecticut.

The other "con" is that Watson is mostly okay, but sometimes he can be a jerk.

"Kristy? Karen? Andrew?"

"Yes, Mom?" It was a Saturday evening, and my mother had invited Watson and his kids over for dinner.

Karen and Andrew and I were crowded into a lawn chair in our backyard. They're good kids. I like them a lot. And I know them well since I've been sitting for them off and on for

3

about nine months, since the time the Baby-sitters Club began. Watson and their mother are divorced, and while they live with their mother, they do spend every other weekend and certain vacations with Watson, and some in-between time, too, if they want. The arrangement is pretty loose.

"Dinner's ready!" called Mom.

"Come on, you guys," I said. "You know what we're having?"

"What?" asked Andrew cautiously. He's a very picky eater.

"We're having spaghetti."

"Oh, yum!" cried Karen.

"Pasketti?" Andrew repeated. "Jody Jones said pasketti is dead worms."

"Ew, ew, ew!" exclaimed Karen.

"Well, Jody Jones is wrong," I told them. "Spaghetti is . . . noodles. That's all."

We entered through the back door of our house and went into the dining room. The table was set for eight. Candles were burning and the lights had been dimmed. A bottle of red wine stood next to Watson's place. The dining room had been transformed into an Italian restaurant.

"This looks great, Mom," I said, "but it's June. We should be eating outside. We're wasting the nice weather."

"Oh, honey," my mother replied. "Eat spaghetti on our laps? That sounds like the start of a Tide commercial. We'll be much better off in here."

I laughed. Ever since Mom got engaged to Watson, she's been in a great mood.

My brothers crowded around the table. (They're never too far off when food is about to be served.)

Karen and Andrew approached them shyly. (Yes, even Karen gets shy sometimes.) I think she's shy around Charlie, Sam, and David Michael because she knows they're going to become her stepbrothers and she wants to make a good impression on them. She knows me a lot better than she knows them because of all the baby-sitting I've done for her and for Andrew.

"Hi, Charlie. Hi, Sam. Hi, David Michael," Karen addressed each one solemnly.

"Hi, kid," replied Charlie. (Charlie is my seventeen-year-old brother. He just got his driver's license.)

Sam, who's fifteen, couldn't answer Karen because he was busy scarfing up olives from a little dish my mother had set on the table next to the pepper grinder.

"Hey, Mom!" I called into the kitchen. "We need an olive refill."

Sam gave me a dirty look.

While we kids stood around waiting for Mom and Watson, who were doing last-minute spaghetti things in the kitchen, Karen and David Michael eyed each other. Mom is afraid there's going to be some trouble between the two of them after the wedding. David Michael is used to being the baby of the family. He's not just the youngest, he's the *much*-youngest. There's a ten-year difference between Charlie and him. There's even a five-and-a-half-year difference between him and me. (I'll be thirteen in August.) But suddenly he's going to acquire a part-time six-year-old sister and four-year-old brother.

Meanwhile, Karen is used to being the oldest. And she's going to acquire *three* part-time older brothers plus me.

Furthermore, Karen and David Michael are so close in age that Mom is sure they're going to be competing for things — toys and privileges and stuff. She wonders whether David Michael will feel cheated because he'll be in public school, while Karen goes to private school. On the other hand, she thinks David Michael would feel resentful if she switched him *out* of the school he's used to.

Things could get pretty messy.

Karen broke the silence in the dining room by gazing around and saying, "Yikes, after Dad and Elizabeth get married, I'm going to have *four* brothers."

"And me," I reminded her. "You'll be my very first sister."

"We better stick together," said Karen. "We're the only girls."

"Oh, yick, yick, yick," said David Michael. "Pew, pew, pew. One sister's enough. Now I'll have two." He made a horrible Halloween face.

"Hey!" exclaimed Karen. "You said a poem, David Michael!"

"I did?"

"Yeah. Say it again."

David Michael tried to repeat his nasty remark, but couldn't remember it.

"Serves you right," I said. "What'd I ever do to you?"

David Michael looked puzzled. Then he smiled. "Nothing!"

I shook my head.

Through all of this, Andrew did not say a word.

Mom and Watson came into the dining room then, Mom carrying a pot of tomato sauce, Watson following with the spaghetti. When everyone had been served, Watson poured wine for Mom and himself.

"Can I have some?" asked Charlie.

Watson looked at Mom. We all knew what the answer would be, but I liked the fact that Watson let Mom say it. For the time being, she was still our boss. The Thomas boss. And Watson knew it.

"When you reach the drinking age," replied Mom pleasantly, "then you may drink."

"But Mom, a year from now I'll be going to college. All the kids — " Charlie stopped. Mom isn't too partial to any sentence that begins with "all the kids."

Charlie gave up. He looked like he might sulk for a while, though.

"Well," Mom said cheerily, "we've set the date."

"What date?" I asked. I twirled a huge mound of spaghetti onto my fork, raised it, and watched the spaghetti slide off.

"The date of the wedding."

"Oh, yeah?" said Sam. He sucked a mouthful of spaghetti in through pursed lips. Andrew watched with interest. Sam never looked up from his plate. "When's the big day?" he asked.

"The third Saturday in September," Mom answered proudly. She was about to make goo-goo eyes at Watson. I've gotten so I can tell when this is going to happen.

"What's a wedding?" asked Andrew suddenly. He had not touched his pasketti.

Mom's goo-goo eyes changed to surprised eyes. She looked from Andrew to Watson and back to Andrew.

"*You* know," Karen told Andrew. "I showed you a whole wedding. Remember when I put on the long white dress and kissed Boo-Boo?" (Boo-Boo is the Brewers' cat.)

Andrew nodded.

"We've talked about the wedding, Andrew," Watson added. "And everyone here is going to be a part of it."

It was my turn to act surprised. "We *are*? I mean, *I* am? *I'm* going to be in the *wedding?*"

"If you want to be," said Mom. "I'd like you to be my bridesmaid."

"Your bridesmaid?" I whispered. "Really? Like in a long, fancy dress with flowers in my hair?" I was awed.

"Since when do you like long, fancy dresses and flowers?" asked Sam.

"Since right now," I replied. "Oh, *Mom!*"

"Is that a yes? You'll be my bridesmaid?"

"It's a YES-YES-YES!" I jumped up and ran around the table to hug my mother.

When I was sitting down again, she went on. "And Charlie, I'd be honored if you'd give me away."

"*Sure*," said Charlie eagerly. (He must have forgotten about the wine.)

"Sam," Watson spoke up, "I'd like you to be my best man."

"And David Michael to be the ringbearer," said Mom.

"What about *me*?" cried Karen.

"How would you like to be the flower girl?" asked Watson. "You'd walk up the aisle in front of Elizabeth and me, carrying a basket of rose petals."

"Oooh," breathed Karen.

"And Andrew can escort you," said Mom. "That means he'll walk beside you."

"What does that make him?" asked Sam. "The flower boy?"

Everyone laughed. Everyone except Andrew. When we calmed down, he said softly, "I don't want to be in the wedding. And I mean it." (I wasn't too surprised. Andrew is terribly shy.)

Watson and Mom looked at each other. "When he means it, he means it — usually," said Watson. He turned to Andrew. "Well, think it over. We'd like you to be in the wedding, but it's up to you, okay?"

10

"Okay."

I didn't give another thought to Andrew all evening. The only thing I could think about was the wedding. I, Kristin Amanda Thomas, was going to be a bridesmaid.

# CHAPTER 2

I have usually found that, in life, good things are followed by bad things. One day you get an A-plus on a spelling test, the next time around you get a C (or worse). A run of good luck is followed by a run of bad luck. Good news is followed by bad news.

It was that way with the wedding.

On Saturday we had all that good wedding news. Mom and Watson had settled on the September date. They'd asked us kids to be part of the ceremony. Mom had even told me later that my wedding shoes could be my first pair of shoes with heels. I couldn't believe it.

That was Saturday.

On Wednesday, just four days later, came the bad stuff. The whole wedding fell apart. In one glump.

My first clue that something was wrong was that Mom was at home when I got there after school. She's almost never home before six o'clock. She has this important job with a big company in Stamford and she works very hard. My brothers and I are used to looking out for ourselves after school.

Needless to say, I was surprised to find Mom sitting at the table in our kitchen at three-thirty in the afternoon. She wasn't doing anything — just sitting there.

"Mom?" I said, as I set my bookbag on the counter. "Are you sick?"

"No, honey, I'm fine," she replied.

"How come you're home? Is David Michael sick?"

"No, no. Everyone's fine. But, well, I just can't believe what happened today."

"Uh-oh," I said. "What?"

"For starters, the company wants to send me on a two-week business trip to Europe."

"Europe!" I shrieked. "Europe? What's wrong with that? London! Paris! Rome! Oh, Mom, can I come? Please? Are you going over the summer? I promise I'll be good. I'll stay out of your way. I won't ask you to buy souvenirs or anything. Just food. *Please?*"

Mom gave me a wry smile. "I'd like nothing better than to take you to Europe, sweetie," she said, "but unfortunately the trip is scheduled during the school year."

It was June. There wasn't much left to the

school year. "You mean you're going *now?*" I cried. "Who'll stay with us?"

Mom shook her head. "I'm not going now. The trip is scheduled for September." She let that sink in. "I'm supposed to be in Vienna on the day of the wedding."

"Oops," I said.

"Oops is right."

"So have an October wedding," I suggested. "Think of it — a fall wedding with the leaves turning. It would be really pretty."

"I did think of it, actually," said Mom. "I was sitting at my desk, mentally adding sleeves to our gowns and changing the flowers from roses to chrysanthemums, when the phone rang. Guess who it was."

I'm not good at guessing games. "I'll never guess, Mom. Who was it?"

"The real estate agent. And guess — wait, I won't make you guess again. Believe it or not, she's already got a buyer for our house."

"Already! You just put the house on the market two days ago. You thought it would take months to sell it. That's great news, Mom!"

"Sort of great. The buyer is desperate. He's in a rush. He's willing to pay what we asked for, which is more than we thought we'd actually get for the house. Here's the catch:

14

He's in such a big hurry that he wants to move his family in by July fifteenth."

"Mom, no! That's next month. It's impossible. Sell the house to someone else."

"I don't think anyone else will pay us this much money."

"Well, what do we need money for? You're marrying Watson."

"Honey, Watson and I and Watson's ex-wife and your father all have various ideas about how to spend our money. It's quite complicated, but for the time being, let's just say that I don't want Watson to feel obliged to finance four extra college educations. The money from the house, half of which, first of all, is your father's, goes toward college for you and your brothers. So the more we make, the better."

"Mom, I'm trying as hard as I can to follow all of this, but what exactly are you saying?"

"I'm saying that Watson and I are going to have to get married at the end of the month so we can move into the Brewers' house two weeks later."

I was stunned. I stared at Mom with my mouth hanging open. David Michael came home, let Louie (our collie) in, sat down in Mom's lap, and still I was openmouthed and speechless.

The phone rang. Mom answered it. It was a friend of hers. They had a long, chatty conversation which ended with Mom saying, "So the upshot is that the wedding will be in two and a half weeks."

"Two and a half weeks," I moaned.

"What's going on?" asked David Michael.

"It's a long story," I told him.

Mom hung up the phone. She seemed awfully calm — too calm.

The next thing I knew, she was going crazy. She leaped to her feet (David Michael jumped out of her lap just in time), held her hands to her head, and cried, "Oh, my lord! How can I plan a whole wedding in two and a half weeks? Two and a half *weeks!* Planning a wedding is like having a baby. You need time to pre*pare* things! You have to talk to the florist, the minister, the dressmaker, the caterer. You have to tell the relatives. You have to *rent chairs!* I can just picture the caterer when I order crab crepes for three hundred. He'll say, 'And what month is the wedding? December?' and I'll say, 'No, it's this month,' and he'll *laugh* at me!"

"Mom — " I started to say.

David Michael tiptoed across the kitchen and held my hand. He stared at Mom, fascinated.

Louie hid under the table.

16

"A tent! We have to rent a tent!" she cried.

"Rent-a-tent, rent-a-tent," chanted David Michael, giggling.

"Mom — "

"We'll hold the wedding in Watson's yard. We'll never be able to rent a hall somewhere for the reception. What if it *rains?!*"

"Mom — "

"Oh, lord — decorations!"

"Mom, why don't you call Watson?" I managed to say.

"I better call Watson," said Mom. (She hadn't heard me.)

Good. I hoped he could calm her down.

Mom went into her bedroom and called Watson privately. When she returned, she looked saner. Sort of. But then she opened up a cabinet and began pulling pots and pans and things out of it. She seemed to be sorting them into piles.

"What are you doing?" I asked her.

"Not only do I have to plan a wedding, I have to get ready to move. This whole house needs to be packed up. We can take the opportunity to clean things out. I bet we haven't cleaned the house out in five years. We can make a big donation to Goodwill."

David Michael began to whine. And even though I'm too old to whine, I joined in.

David Michael started with, "But I don't *wanna* move. I wanna stay *he-ere*." (David Michael is a champion whiner. Anybody who can turn a one-syllable word into a two-syllable word is good — very good.)

I added, "I want one more summer here. I don't *wanna* leave yet."

Mom pulled her head out of the cabinet. Very slowly she turned around to face us. She didn't say one word, just looked at David Michael and me.

"Uh-oh," said David Michael under his breath. He apologized quickly. "Sorry, Mom." Then he hustled out of the kitchen with Louie at his heels.

Mom was still looking at me. But I wasn't about to apologize. I was sorry I'd whined at her, but I was still upset about the move. "You said we weren't moving until the fall," I told her. "You said we'd still be here this summer."

"Those weren't promises, Kristy," replied Mom. "That's simply what I thought was going to happen."

"But Mom, no fair. I don't want to spend this summer at Watson's."

"You'll be spending next summer at Watson's," she pointed out. "And the one after that and the one after that."

"I know. That's why I want this summer

*here*, with my friends. One last summer with Mary Anne and the Baby-sitters Club and Jamie Newton and the Pikes and — and in my own room . . ." I trailed off.

"I'm sorry, honey," said Mom. "This is the way things are, fair or otherwise."

"*Boy*," I exclaimed. I stomped upstairs.

When I got to my room I closed my door. I considered slamming it, but I wasn't really angry. I was sad.

I sat down at my desk and looked out the window. There are two windows in my room. One faces the front yard. The other faces the side. Mary Anne Spier's house is next door, and I can look right into her bedroom from that side window.

She wasn't there that day. She was baby-sitting for Jenny Prezzioso. I was kind of glad, because I just wanted to be able to stare and think. If Mary Anne had seen me at the window, she would have wanted to talk.

A lot of things, both good and bad, have happened at those windows. For years, every night after Mary Anne's strict father had made her go to bed, we used to stand at the windows with flashlights and signal each other with a secret flashing code Mary Anne had made up. (We don't have to do that anymore, though, because Mr. Spier has changed. Now he lets

Mary Anne talk on the phone at night like a normal person.)

When Mary Anne and I had fights, I knew I could always get to her by pulling my window shade down. It was like not speaking to her. When we weren't fighting, which was most of the time, we would string a paper-cup telephone between our rooms, or sail paper airplanes with messages on them through the windows. What was I ever going to do without Mary Anne next door?

And what was I going to do in a new bedroom? The room I was in had been my bedroom since the day my parents brought me home from the hospital. It was fixed up just the way I wanted it. Over at Watson's, I could have my pick of bedrooms. I could be on the second or third floor. I could be near my brothers or away from them. I could have a big room or a not-so-big room, but it didn't matter. It wouldn't be the same. No matter what my room was like, I wouldn't be able to look out the window and into Mary Anne's room. "My" room would never feel like *my* room.

I tried to picture all the bedrooms I had ever seen at the Brewers'. Maybe there was one like mine — with a window facing front, another window facing the side, the closet opposite the front window, the door opposite the side window. Maybe I would take that room and arrange my furniture in it just the way it's arranged now. It wouldn't be the same, but it would help.

"Kristy?" I heard Mom call.

I opened my door. "What?" I shouted back.

"I need you here."

· "All right." I went slowly downstairs.

Mom was sitting at the kitchen table with papers spread out all around her. Before I asked her what she wanted, I peeked in the cabinet she'd started to clear out. Everything had been thrown back in. I guessed the packing was going to wait until later.

"Can you help me make some lists, sweetie?" said Mom. "We've got to start listing *every*thing if we're going to pull off this wedding: things to do, things to buy, people to call. . . ."

"Okay," I said.

"First we'll list people to invite to the wedding. I'll go through our address book and you write down the names I call out."

When we were done, Mom looked at the list I had made. "Hmm. An awful lot of these people are from out of state, and a lot of them have a lot of children. It's a good thing they'll only be in town a night or two."

We started in on some other lists. Weddings

sure are complicated. I didn't know they take so much work. By five-thirty, when it was time for a meeting of the Baby-sitters Club, I was overwhelmed. I realized why Mom had gone crazy earlier.

I began to feel sort of sorry for her.

# CHAPTER 3

Mom had kept me so busy with the wedding lists that by the time I dashed across the street to Claudia's house, it was five-thirty-six and I was the last to arrive. As club president, that was not an ideal situation. However, since the others were all there already, I took advantage of the situation to get a good, long look at them. Since I knew I'd be moving soon, I felt I wanted to do that, even though I'd still see them at our meetings and in school.

Claudia Kishi, our vice-president and a junk-food addict, was prowling around her room, trying to remember where she'd hidden a large bag of M&M's. She was wearing one of her usual outrageous outfits: a black leotard and skintight red pants under a white shirt that was so big it looked like a lab coat. Claudia's a wonderful artist and she had decorated the shirt herself, covering it with designs painted in acrylic. She had pinned her long, black hair back at the sides with red clips.

Mary Anne Spier, secretary of the club and my best friend, was sitting on the floor, leaning against Claudia's bed. Her wavy brown hair had recently been brushed and looked shiny and full. Until a few months ago, she had always worn it in two braids. I still wasn't used to seeing it loose. As secretary, Mary Anne was in charge of the Baby-sitters Club Record Book, where we write down appointments and keep track of our clients' addresses and things.

Stacey, our treasurer, was sitting cross-legged on the bed with the envelope containing the club dues in front of her. Like Claudia, Stacey enjoys looking good. She enjoys putting together outfits and she enjoys shopping. So does her mother, who has time for such things. (I'm happy in jeans and a T-shirt.) But Stacey is from New York City, where shopping is the official city sport. Stacey's blonde hair was permed, and what with that, her purple nail polish, and her Swatch accessories, she looked, well, kind of like a thirteen-year-old Madonna. (If Claudia weren't Japanese, she'd look a little like Madonna, too.)

Seated on the floor next to Mary Anne was the newest member of the Baby-sitters Club and Mary Anne's other best friend (I'm the first one). Dawn Schafer had been named our official alternate officer, which means that she's familiar with the job of every club officer and can substitute for anyone who can't make a meeting. Dawn has the most amazing hair I've ever seen. It's straight and fine and hangs down past her waist, and it's so light I couldn't even call it blonde. It's almost white. It's the color of sunlight or bleached straw. I hope she never cuts it or changes it.

"Hi, everybody," I said.

"Hi!" replied the members of the Baby-sitters Club.

"Want some?" asked Claudia. She'd just found the M&M's in a box under her bed labeled ARTWORK: STILL LIFS AND PORTRITS. (Claudia is a terrible speller.) She tore a corner off the bag and motioned for me to hold my hands out. I did, and took a few.

"Sorry I'm late," I said, settling myself in Claudia's director's chair. "Any calls yet?"

"One," Stacey answered. "I have a feeling it was Sam. The person said, 'Hello, this is Marmee March. I need a sitter for Amy tonight, someone who has experience with little women.' "

I scowled. "Sam, all right. He never takes this club seriously."

"Oh, well," said Mary Anne, holding out

her hands as Claudia went by her with the M&M's. "Who cares?"

"Yeah," I said. "Well, we better get down to business. Have you all been reading the notebook?" (We also keep a notebook in which we write up each baby-sitting job we go on. Everyone is supposed to read the book a couple of times a week so we know what's going on with the kids we sit for.)

The others nodded.

"How much money is in the treasury, Stace?" I asked next.

"Seventeen dollars and twenty-five cents."

"Oh, that's good! Can you guys think of anything we need?"

The money in the treasury doesn't come from what we earn baby-sitting (at least not directly), but from our club dues, and we use it to buy things we need for the club as well as to give ourselves a little treat every now and then, such as a slumber party.

"I don't think we need anything," replied Claudia. "Maybe we should have a party — an end-of-school party or something."

"Maybe," I murmured.

"Kristy?" asked Mary Anne. "Anything wrong? You seem sort of quiet."

I might as well get it over with. "I've got good news and bad news," I replied.

"Uh-oh," said Dawn.

"The good news is that I'm going to be a bridesmaid in Mom's wedding."

"Oooh," the other members of the club sighed happily.

"The bad news is that the wedding's in two and a half weeks and we're moving in July."

*"What?"* cried Mary Anne, jumping up. "You can't! You can't move in July!"

"I tried to tell Mom the same thing," I said, "but she wouldn't listen. She has all sorts of reasons for selling the house right now. They're too complicated to explain."

Mary Anne looked like she might cry, but Dawn couldn't get past the wedding part. "You're going to be a bridesmaid, Kristy? Oh, you're so lucky!"

At that moment, Claudia's phone rang. Usually we all lunge for it, but we were so caught up with the news of the wedding that it rang twice before Stacey reached lazily for the receiver and said, "Hello. Baby-sitters Club."

As soon as she said that, though, we went into action. Mary Anne opened up our club record book and turned to the appointment pages so she could see our baby-sitting schedules; the rest of us paid attention.

When Stacey hung up she said, "That was Dr. Johanssen. She needs a sitter for Charlotte after school on Friday, from three-thirty to five-thirty."

"Well," said Mary Anne, "Dawn and I are the only ones who don't have jobs then."

"But Jeff and I are going over to our grandparents' house that afternoon," Dawn spoke up, "so you can sit for Charlotte, Mary Anne." (Jeff is Dawn's younger brother.)

Mary Anne penciled the job into our calendar.

Then Stacey called Dr. Johanssen back to let her know she had a sitter. When she hung up the phone, she said, "Tell us about the good news first, Kristy. Tell us about being a bridesmaid."

"Well," I said, "actually, I've known about that since Saturday, but I didn't say anything because . . . because. . . ." How could I explain that the reason I hardly ever talked about the wedding was that, deep down, I still wasn't sure I wanted Mom and Watson to get married? The girls would never understand. They'd all met Watson and they liked him. They'd all baby-sat for Karen and Andrew, and they thought they were adorable and wonderful. They'd all have swapped their own houses for Watson's mansion in a second. And Mary Anne, whose widowed father has been going out with Dawn's divorced mother, would have died with pleasure if *those two* had decided to get married.

Finally I said, "I didn't say anything because we still thought the wedding was going to be in September and it seemed so far off."

Mary Anne looked at me skeptically.

"But *tell* us about it," Stacey persisted. "Like, what are you going to wear?"

Even I had to admit that what I was going to wear was glamorous and exciting. "Well," I said. . . .

And just then the phone rang again.

Business first.

"Hello. Baby-sitters Club," said Dawn. "Oh, hi. . . . Yes. . . . Yes. . . . Just Claire and Margo? Okay, I'll call you right back." She hung up. "That was Mrs. Pike. She needs a sitter next Tuesday afternoon, but only for the two little ones" (Claire and Margo Pike have six older brothers and sisters) "from three-thirty until six."

Mary Anne looked in the book. "Let's see. Kristy, you'll be watching David Michael then. Claudia, you have an art class. And I'm sitting for Jenny Prezzioso. Dawn or Stacey?"

"I've got to see the doctor in New York on Tuesday," said Stacey. "We'll be gone the whole day."

"Everything all right?" asked Claudia.

"Yup," replied Stacey. "Just a checkup." (Stacey has diabetes. She's on a strict diet — none of Claudia's junk food allowed — and the doctors and her parents keep a sharp eye on her.)

Dawn called Mrs. Pike back to say that she'd be sitting.

"Bridesmaid gown," said Stacey the second Dawn had taken her hand off the receiver.

"Okay," I said with a smile. Mom and I had finally decided on exactly what we'd all be wearing. "It's going to be a long gown — "

"Oooh."

" — with short sleeves and a ribbon sash above my waist. Mom says that'll make me look taller — and older."

"What color?" asked Mary Anne.

"Whatever color I want, as long as Karen agrees to it. She's going to be the flower girl, and her dress is supposed to look like a younger version of mine. I mean, it won't be long, and the sash will be at her waist, but it has to be the same material."

"I think you should choose pink," said Dawn.

I wrinkled up my nose. "Too cutesy."

"Green," said Claudia.

"For a wedding?"

"How about yellow?" suggested Mary Anne.

"Pale yellow. That would be pretty for the summer. And you and Karen both look good in yellow."

Everyone agreed that yellow was the best choice for my dress.

"What about your shoes?" said Claudia.

"Hey!" I said. "Get this. Mom said I can wear heels — "

"Oooh."

" — and we're going to buy these special shoes that you can dye to match your dress."

"Oooh."

In spite of myself, I was beginning to feel excited again. "Did I tell you that all us kids are going to be in the wedding?"

"Really?" squealed the others.

"Well, everyone except Andrew. He's shy about things like that. Karen's going to be the flower girl, like I said. Charlie's going to give Mom away, Sam's going to be the best man, and David Michael's going to be the ring-bearer."

Everyone began talking at once: "Oh, you're kidding!" "I wish *I* could be in a wedding."

"When did you say it will be?" asked Claudia.

"In just two and a half weeks. On a Saturday. A week after school is over."

Claudia sighed with joy. "I can't stand it!

Only a week and a half of school left and then . . . *summer!*" (As you can probably tell, Claudia does not like school.)

"A week and a half!" Stacey exclaimed. "Gosh, it crept up on me. In New York, I went to a private school. Summer vacation began right after Memorial Day. I thought I'd never last until June nineteenth. But now it's almost here. What happens at the end of school? Anything special?"

"The Final Fling," Claudia replied.

"The Final Fling?"

"It's the last dance of the year," I told her.

"And the usual stuff," added Mary Anne. "Room and teacher assignments for eighth grade."

"Report cards," said Claudia, making a face that looked as if she'd accidentally taken a swallow of sour milk.

"Let's decide what we're going to wear to the dance," suggested Stacey.

"I'm not going," Mary Anne said immediately.

"But you don't have to be asked to the Final Fling," I pointed out. "You can just go."

"I'm still not going. I don't like dances."

"Well, I'm going," said Claudia.

"With Trevor?" I asked. Trevor Sandbourne was the love of Claudia's life last fall.

Claudia looked at me as if I'd asked if she was going to the dance with Winnie-the-Pooh. "*Trevor?* No. Trevor's probably dating his own poetry at this point. That's all he cares about."

We giggled.

"If Alan Gray asks me, I'll go," I said. "I still think he's a pest, but he can be a lot of fun."

"I'll go," said Stacey, "with or without Pete." (Pete Black was part of Stacey and Claudia's crowd. He and Stacey had gone to several dances together.) "I think he likes Dorianne now. Are you going, Dawn?"

Dawn frowned. "I have to decide."

We began to discuss what we'd wear. The phone rang with several more calls. By the time our meeting was over, I was more excited about the Final Fling than the wedding.

# CHAPTER 4

The Final Fling came and went. I did go with Alan Gray. He was himself — fifty percent pesty and fifty percent fun. Claudia went with Austin Bentley, a new boy in school, and Stacey went with Pete after all. (Dorianne made wicked faces at them during the dance.) Dawn decided not to go. Mr. Spier had offered to take Mary Anne and the Schafers out for pizza, and Dawn and Mary Anne never turned down a chance to see their parents together.

The last day of school came and went, too, and before I knew it, I was home that afternoon, hugging a garbage bag full of junk I'd cleaned out of my locker.

It was one week and one day before the wedding. Mom had decided to take the following week off from work to get ready for the big day. To make up for it, she'd said she would have to work extra hard ahead of time.

So when I came home to find Mom sitting at our kitchen table looking hysterical, I was especially surprised.

"Mom!" I exclaimed. "Today was your last day at the office before the wedding. I thought you'd be there forever. How come you're home already?" I began checking the contents of the refrigerator.

Sam appeared in the kitchen doorway. "That's a touchy question, Kristy. I just asked her the same thing, and you know what she said?"

"What?" I asked. I took an orange out of the fridge.

"I can't repeat it in mixed company."

I stuck my tongue out at Sam. But his comment rated a smile from my mother.

"Oh, Sam, it wasn't that bad," said Mom.

"Don't tell me," I said, suddenly inspired. "Let me take a guess. The wedding's in five days and we're moving in two weeks."

"No," said Mom with another smile.

"The wedding's tomorrow and we're moving on Wednesday?"

"No."

"The wedding's in five minutes and we're moving tonight?"

"No. But how about this? Sheila and Kendall" (they're Watson's ex-wife and her new husband) "called Watson to say that they're going to England for most of next week, and leaving Karen and Andrew with Watson."

"So?" said Sam and I.

"And Aunt Colleen and Uncle Wallace decided to come down on Sunday to help me with the wedding next week."

"Goody," I said. Colleen and Wallace are my favorite aunt and uncle.

"They're bringing Ashley, Berk, Grace, and Peter with them."

"Oh." (They're my cousins.)

"And Aunt Theo and Uncle Neal also called to let me know they're arriving on Sunday to help with the wedding. They're bringing Emma, Beth, and Luke."

"Oh." (More cousins.)

"*And —* " Mom went on.

"Uh-oh," said Sam and I at the same time.

"Tom Fielding, Watson's best friend — they haven't seen each other in a couple of years — is coming Saturday evening. With his wife, and Katherine, Patrick, Maura, and Tony. I think."

"More kids?" I asked.

Mom nodded.

"Where," I said cautiously, "are all these people going to stay?"

"Our relatives are staying at the Ramada Inn

in Shelbyville, and Watson's friends are staying with him." Mom paused. "However," she continued, "the adults are all going to be helping at the Brewers' during the day next week. That means that thirteen children are going to be running around, too. Fourteen, if I have to bring David Michael with me."

I raised my eyebrows.

"Holy . . ." Sam started to say, and then trailed off. "Fourteen? Are you sure?"

I counted them off. "Ashley, Berk, Grace, Peter, Emma, Beth, Luke, Andrew, Karen, David Michael, and — who are Watson's friend's kids?"

"Katherine, Patrick, Maura, and Tony," said Mom.

"Yup. That's fourteen."

Sam let out a low whistle.

"Next week," said my mother, "I need adults to help me cook, arrange flowers, set up chairs, shop, and do about a hundred other things. I do not need fourteen children underfoot."

Mom buried her head in her hands. "I will never pull this wedding off. Never. We're not going to get a thing done. We'll spend all next week breaking up fights over Tinker Toys and deciding who gets the last cookie."

In a flash, a brilliant idea came to me. (My best ideas come in flashes.)

"Hey, Mom, today was the last day of school," I pointed out.

"Oh, I know, honey. I'm sorry. How was it? How was your report card?"

"I got straight A's again, but that's not what I mean. I mean that school's *over*. Starting right now, I have nothing to do — except baby-sit."

"Kristy, you're a good, responsible baby-sitter, but even you can't take care of fourteen children."

"No, but the Baby-sitters Club can. There are five of us. The kids could come over here during the day."

"Oh, brother," exclaimed Sam. It was his turn to sit down and bury his head in his hands.

"That way," I said, "the adults could work at the Brewers' without any interruptions."

"Well, Kristy," said Mom, "that might be the solution."

"I have to check with the other club members, of course, and we might have to cancel some appointments, but I think we could do it. Would you really hire the whole Baby-sitters Club for the whole week?"

"I really would. And if the girls would really sit from nine to five Monday through Friday, Watson and I would really pay the club, let's see . . ." (Mom did some fast mental arith-metic) ". . . six hundred dollars."

*"What!"* exploded Sam.

"That's three dollars an hour apiece, which comes to a hundred and twenty dollars for each of you for the week."

My jaw almost fell off. A hundred and twenty dollars in just one week!

"Mom, I'll give you a bargain," said Sam. "For just five hundred dollars, *I'll* take care of the kids."

"All fourteen of them? No way. Besides, I believe you already have a summer job."

"I know, I know." Sam was going to deliver groceries for the A&P. He had done it the summer before. It didn't pay too badly, but five or six hundred dollars *was* an awful lot of money, even divided five ways. No wonder Sam was jealous.

"Don't you think you're overpaying them?" he asked.

"It's only three dollars an hour," replied Mom. "That's slightly more than what they usually charge, but there are fourteen children involved. How much do *you* make?"

"A little more than that per hour — but I get tips," said Sam.

"Kristy! Kristy!"

David Michael came crashing through the front door and into the kitchen. He was loaded down with rolled-up artwork, his lunch box, a shopping bag, and an envelope holding old papers and worksheets. "Oh, Mom, you're home already. Hey, guess what, everybody!" He dropped all his stuff on the floor, jumped over it, and thrust a piece of paper across the table at us.

Mom took it. I peered at it. A large gold star was glued to the top.

" 'Citizenship Award,' " Mom read. " 'This certifies that David Michael Thomas has been chosen best citizen of the year in Mr. Bowman's room, by his peers.' "

"That means the other kids," David Michael explained.

"Duh," said Sam. (Mom hushed him with one look.)

She turned to David Michael. "Honey, congratulations!" she said. "We'll have to frame this."

"They voted on me," David Michael told us breathlessly, "and Mr. Bowman wrote my name on the blank and gave it to me and said I should be proud. Can we put this with the other awards?"

(There's this wall in the den that's covered

with awards Charlie and Sam and I have won. There's also a table filled with trophies. Until today, David Michael didn't have any awards or trophies, so this was a big deal for him.)

"Of course," said Mom. "As soon as it's framed."

Mom began helping David Michael put away all the junk he'd brought home from school. Sam and I drifted onto the back porch.

"You know," I said, stretching out in a wicker chair and putting my feet up on the table, "in about two weeks, there isn't going to be an awards wall anymore. Everything will be packed away for the move."

"Yeah, I thought of that," said Sam. He eased himself into a lawn chair and ran his fingers through his curly hair. "Poor kid." (I guessed he meant David Michael.)

"Do you think Mom'll put up our awards wall and the trophy table at Watson's?" I asked.

Sam shrugged.

"Hey, Sam, um . . . what do you think about going to the Brewers'? I mean, I know you like Watson, but . . . it's just . . . everything's going to be so different."

"I don't mind. I don't have to change schools. That's really important. None of us has to change schools. Did you know that Mom and

Watson have to pay to let you stay at Stoneybrook Middle School instead of switching to Kelsey Middle School?"

"You're kidding. How come?"

"Because Kelsey is closer to Watson's, so technically you should go there when you change school districts. But the officials make an exception if you pay a fee. Mom has to pay for David Michael to stay at Stoneybrook Elementary School, too. It doesn't make any difference to Charlie and me, though, since there's only one high school."

"I didn't know all this," I said.

"Mom and Watson are trying to make the move as easy on us as possible."

"I guess so. But Sam, we still aren't Watson's kids, you and Charlie and David Michael and I. Even though we'll be living over there, we won't be his kids. Just his stepkids."

"What are you getting at, Kristy?"

"Well, for instance, if Watson was my real father, and he was still a millionaire, I could ask him for big things, like a VCR for my bedroom. But since he'll only be my step, can I ask him for *any*thing? I mean, say I need to borrow a couple of dollars and Mom's not around. Could I ask Watson? Mom said something about Watson not having to be responsible for our college educations."

"There's a big difference between four college tuitions and two dollars," said Sam.

"I know. But there's a big difference between four tuitions and a VCR, too, and I wouldn't ask him for a VCR. Where do you draw the line? In what ways is he our father?"

"Those are heavy questions," said another voice.

Charlie had come home. He joined Sam and me on the porch.

"I've been doing a lot of thinking," I told them. "You know how I don't like guessing games. Well, I don't like surprises, either. I like to know what's going to happen."

"But no one knows what's going to happen, Kristy," said Charlie, the voice of reason. "Even Mom and Watson don't really know what to expect."

"I feel like we're in a movie," I said.

*"The Bride of Frankenstein?"* asked Sam.

"No, not *The Bride of Frankenstein*." I stuck my tongue out at Sam. Fifteen-year-old brothers are a real drag. It's too bad boys can't skip from fourteen right to sixteen or seventeen.

*"I Married a Witch?"* Sam guessed.

*"No!* It's just . . . well . . . think about it. Mom and Dad get divorced, Mom meets new guy, new guy has two kids, new guy turns out to be millionaire, Mom and new guy get

married, we move to mansion. But that doesn't mean it has a happy ending."

"Yeah, stay tuned for Part Two," said Charlie. "I know what you mean. It's hard to believe."

"And scary."

"But," said Sam, turing serious, "we can make it work."

"You think so?" I asked hopefully. I looked at my brothers.

They nodded.

"Then stay tuned for Part Two!" I said.

CHAPTER
5

The next day, I called the first emergency meeting of the Baby-sitters Club that we'd had in a long time. It wasn't easy keeping my news a secret, but I managed not to say a word about the fourteen children or the six hundred dollars until Mary Anne, Claudia, Stacey, Dawn, and I had gathered in Claudia's room.

"What's this all about?" asked Stacey. She was lying on her back across Claudia's bed with her head hanging over the side, brushing her hair.

"Yeah, an emergency on the first day of summer vacation?" said Claudia from the end of her bed where she was leafing through a fashion magazine.

"Well, maybe it's not a true emergency," I said, "but it's very important and we have to take care of it right away."

"Did something happen?" asked Dawn.

"Just this," I said. "You all know that the wedding is a week from today."

"Oh, and I can't wait!" exclaimed Mary Anne. "I know exactly what I'm going to wear."

"I'm dying to see your bridesmaid gown," added Stacey.

The wedding was going to be on the big side. Mom and Watson had each asked a lot of guests, and they had let my brothers and me invite some people, too. Of course, my guests were the Spiers, the Kishis, the McGills, and the Schafers. They were all going to be there.

"Well, anyway, it's in a week," I said again. "And since Mom has so much to do and so little time to do it in, my relatives and some friends of Watson's decided to give her a hand."

"That's nice," said Stacey.

"It is," I agreed, "except that they all live out of town and they're all arriving by Monday — with their kids. Mom realized that while the adults are working on the wedding this week, there are going to be fourteen children who need looking after."

"Fourteen!" exclaimed Claudia.

"Yup. Seven of my cousins, four kids who belong to Watson's friend, plus Karen, Andrew, and David Michael. At first Mom thought the kids would just have to hang around Watson's while the adults are working, but she knows they're going to be in the way. So I sort of made a suggestion."

"What?" asked Dawn suspiciously.

"I suggested that the kids come over to my house every day this week and we'll baby-sit for them. That way the grown-ups will be able to get their work done."

"Us? Take care of fourteen children?" squeaked Mary Anne.

"Mom said that if we baby-sit for them from nine to five every day, she and Watson will pay us each . . . *one hundred and twenty dollars.*"

I looked around the room, expecting something to happen. I thought for sure someone would screech or gasp or fall off the bed.

Nothing.

I gave them a few moments to recover. Then I broke the stunned silence by saying, "That's six hundred dollars all together."

Finally I got a reaction.

In a teeny-tiny voice, Claudia said, "One hundred and twenty *dollars?* With one hundred and twenty dollars, I could buy one hundred and twenty bags of peppermints. That's about a year's supply."

Everyone began to laugh.

"You could buy three hundred packages of Twinkies," said Stacey.

"Or one thousand two hundred jawbreakers," I said with a giggle.

"Four hundred packs of gum," suggested Dawn.

"Sixty cartons of ice cream," said Mary Anne.

"Ice cream," said Claudia, "is one thing I've never been able to hide in my room."

There was another pause.

"You're serious about this, right?" Dawn asked me.

"Of course I'm serious," I replied. "Mom's in a real bind. We didn't figure on this happening. And with everyone coming from out of town. . . ." I shrugged. "We have to do something."

"And your mom thinks we can handle it?" Mary Anne ventured timidly.

"Yes. So do I," I said. "It works out to two or three kids for each of us. We can do that easily."

"But fourteen at once," said Mary Anne.

"A hundred and twenty dollars each," Claudia reminded her.

"What do you say?" I asked the members of the group.

I looked at Claudia. She nodded emphati-

48

cally. I looked at Dawn and Stacey. They nodded, too.

"Mary Anne?" I asked.

She hesitated. Then she nodded as well.

"All *right!*" I cried. "Now look, you guys, we have some work to do. Nine to five means all day, every day next week. A couple of times I'm going to have to leave for dress fittings and wedding things, but otherwise we'll have to stay at my house with the kids. We better see if we have any jobs lined up next week. Mary Anne, can you check our calendar?"

Mary Anne opened the record book to the appointment section. "Let's see," she said. "This isn't too bad. Kristy, you're supposed to sit for Jamie Newton on Tuesday. I'm supposed to sit for Jenny Prezzioso Wednesday evening. I can still do that, I guess. Stacey, you're supposed to sit for Charlotte on Thursday, and we have several things lined up for David Michael and for Karen and Andrew, but those aren't a problem because we're going to be sitting for them, anyway."

"Hmm," I said. "It isn't very good business, but we'll have to call the Newtons and the Johanssens and cancel. Unless . . ." I went on thoughtfully.

"What?" asked Dawn.

"Maybe the kids could just come over to my house. What difference will one more make when we're already watching fourteen?"

"That's true," said Stacey.

I picked up the phone. "I'll call Mrs. Newton," I said, "then you call Dr. Johanssen, Stace."

I explained the situation to Mrs. Newton, who was not only understanding, but enthusiastic. She said she thought the experience would be good for Jamie. He was starting nursery school in the fall and needed to get used to other children.

Then Stacey called Charlotte's mother. "Dr. Johanssen?" she said. "Hi, it's Stacey. Listen, I'm calling about next Thursday. I — what? . . . Oh. . . . Oh, sure. . . . No, it's no problem. Not at all. I'll see you some other time. Say hi to Charlotte. Okay. . . . Okay. . . . 'Bye." She turned to us with a smile. "Well, I got out of that one. Dr. Johanssen was just about to call us to cancel. Her schedule at the hospital got switched around, so she doesn't need me on Thursday."

"Great!" I said. "Does anyone have anything else to cancel? Dentist appointments? Claudia, art classes?"

They shook their heads.

"All right," I went on, "now we better do some planning for next week. First, let me tell you about the kids — their ages and stuff."

"I'm going to take notes while you talk," Mary Anne spoke up.

"Good idea. Okay, we'll start with my cousins. First, there are the Millers — Ashley, Berk, Grace, and Peter. Ashley is . . . I think she just turned nine. Berk's about six."

"Boy or girl?" Mary Anne interrupted.

"Boy," I answered. "Grace is five, and Peter's three."

"Okay," said Mary Anne.

"Then there are the Meiners. Luke is ten, Emma is eight, I think, and Beth is about a year old."

"Okay."

"And then there are those kids of Watson's friend. I don't know anything about them. Maybe I better call Watson," I said.

I dialed Watson's number.

"Hello?" a small voice answered.

"Hi, Karen," I said. "It's Kristy."

"Hi, Kristy! Oh, guess what! Daddy took me shopping today. I got shoes for the wedding and they're very, very beautiful. They're black and shiny and they have a strap that buckles around my ankle."

"Oh, lucky girl! I can't wait to see them. I don't have shoes yet. Listen, Karen, is your daddy there?"

"Yes, he is. But Kristy, Ben Brewer's ghost broke a vase in the living room today. It was really scary."

Karen went on about the ghost for a while, then finally I was able to talk to Watson. When I got off the phone, I said, "All right. Watson's friends are the Fieldings, and the kids are young. Katherine's the oldest. She's five. Patrick is three and Maura's two. Tony is the baby. He's only eight months old."

"Hmm," said Mary Anne. "Let me just add David Michael, Karen, and Andrew to my list." She scribbled away. Then she looked up. "Well, I count seven girls and seven boys, one ten-year-old, two six-year-olds, one nine-year-old, one eight-year-old, a four-year-old, one seven-year-old, two five-year-olds, two three-year-olds, a one-year-old, a two-year-old, and a baby — Tony."

"Gosh, it sounds like kind of a handful when you put it that way," said Dawn. She and the others began to look worried.

"But we'll manage," I said. "You know, maybe we should divide the kids into age groups, organize your list according to age, oldest to youngest."

Mary Anne began writing busily. "Okay," she said after a minute.

Mary Anne's list looked like this:

| | |
|---|---|
| Luke — 10 | Katherine — 5 |
| Ashley — 9 | Andrew — 4 |
| Emma — 8 | Peter — 3 |
| David Michael — 7 | Patrick — 3 |
| Berk — 6 | Maura — 2 |
| Karen — 6 | Beth — 1 |
| Grace — 5 | Tony — 8 months |

"All right," I said. I borrowed Mary Anne's pen and drew four lines, one under Emma, one under Karen, one under Andrew, and one under Maura. "Look at this, everybody. Now we have five groups of kids, one group for each of us. The top group is the oldest kids, and the bottom is the babies. There are three kids in each group except the last. I think whoever has the babies will have her hands full with just two. Diapers and everything."

"We better decide right now who will be in charge of which group," said Dawn.

"Okay," I agreed. "Does anybody especially want the oldest kids?"

Stacey's hand shot up.

I wrote her name next to the top group. Then I asked, "Does anybody especially want the babies?"

Mary Anne raised her hand.

I wrote her name by the babies. Before I could ask who wanted David Michael's group, Claudia said, "I don't really care which kids I have. I like any age."

"Me, too," said Dawn.

"Me, too," I said. So I assigned Dawn to the six- and seven-year-olds, Claudia to the two- and three-year-olds, and gave myself Grace, Katherine, and Andrew. "Andrew feels most comfortable with me," I said. "And also on Tuesday, Jamie Newton will fit right into that age group, and I think he should be my responsibility."

"Hey!" said Mary Anne. "You know what we should do to help keep the groups straight? We should call them the red group, the blue group, or whatever we want, and make, like, red nametags for Stacey's kids, blue tags for Dawn's kids, or something. That way the children will know what group they're in, and we'll be able to spot our kids easily. It'll help us learn their names, too. Kristy, you know most of them, but the rest of us only know Karen, Andrew, and David Michael. And nobody knows the Fieldings."

"Terrific!" cried Claudia enthusiastically, and the rest of us agreed with her.

So Claudia rummaged through her art supplies and found scissors, construction paper, and string. We made red star nametags for Luke, Ashley, and Emma; bluebird tags for David Michael, Berk, and Karen; yellow suns for Grace, Katherine, and Andrew; green dinosaurs for Peter, Patrick, and Maura; and pink hearts for Beth and Tony, the babies.

"Now we should make tags for ourselves," Stacey pointed out. "The group leaders should have tags like their kids'. Then the older children will be able to read our names, and the younger ones at least will be able to figure out who their leader is by matching the tags."

So we made five more nametags. When we were done, we attached all the tags to string, except for Beth and Tony's, which we decided to safety-pin to them.

Claudia then announced that it was time for a high-energy snack, so she rustled up a Snickers bar (from the drawer of her jewelry box), a package of Ring Dings (from the STILL LIFS AND PORTRITS box), and a roll of Life Savers (from her pocket). For Dawn, who often prefers healthier food, and for Stacey, she went to the kitchen and got a box of crackers and some fruit. When she returned, she was with her grandmother, Mimi, who was carrying a tray of sodas for us.

"Hello, girls," said Mimi in her gentle voice. "You seem to be working very hard."

Claudia told her what we were doing.

"Oh, my," said Mimi softly. "Fourteen children! Next week, while your mother is busy, Kristy, and your parents are at work," Mimi nodded to Claudia and Mary Anne, "you must be sure to call on me if you need anything. I will be here at home. You must let me know if you have any problems. I will be happy to help out."

"Thanks, Mimi," I said. "That's really good to know."

"It sure is," said Mary Anne, jumping up to kiss Mimi's cheek.

I could tell Mary Anne was still a little nervous about what we were going to be doing. But she loves Mimi, and if anybody could make her feel better, Mimi could.

Mimi is special to all of us.

When Mimi was gone, I said, "You know, you guys, taking care of fourteen children is kind of like teaching school or running a play group. Maybe we should think of some activities for our kids."

"Yeah, different groups can do different things," said Dawn.

"We could take them to the elementary school playground," suggested Stacey.

"Do art projects," said Claudia.

"I can even take the babies on walks," said Mary Anne.

We were all starting to get excited. We talked and planned and made lists. We couldn't wait for Monday.

# CHAPTER 6

*Wedding Countdown:*
*Sunday — six days to go*

Sunday is my favorite day of the week, summer or winter, for one reason: I get to sleep late.

That's why, when Mom came into my room the next morning, I was not at all pleased.

She opened my door and began pulling up my shades and straightening the things on my dresser, humming all the while.

"Come on, Miss Sleepyhead," she said finally. "Rise and shine."

I scrunched my pillow over my face to block out the light. "Mo-om," I complained. "Why are you doing this to me? What time is it?"

"Eight o'clock."

"Eight o'clock!" I figured she wouldn't be bothering me unless it was at least ten.

"All your brothers are up already."

"But I won't have another chance to sleep late until next Sunday. That's *after* the wedding." I tried to make "after the wedding" sound farther away than it really was, like when you say, "See you next year" on December 31st.

"Honey, I need you today. This is the countdown to the wedding. Only six days left. Aunt Colleen and Uncle Wallace, and Aunt Theo and Uncle Neal are arriving today. They're going to the motel first, but then they're coming over here. They'll probably stay for dinner. And Nannie is going to come over. She wants to measure you again."

Nannie is Mom's mother. She lives in an apartment about forty-five minutes away from us. Nannie is really great. She's in her seventies, but she does all sorts of things. She goes bowling, she gardens, she volunteers at the hospital, she's a terrific cook — and she sews.

Nannie had offered to make my bridesmaid gown and Karen's flower girl dress. She had already taken Karen and me shopping, and we had chosen the patterns and material. Every so often, she needed to measure us.

"Is Nannie going to stay for dinner?" I asked.

"I think so," said Mom. "I'm sure she'll want to see your cousins."

Ashley, Berk, Grace, Peter, Emma, Beth,

and Luke are Nannie's grandchildren, too, of course, and since they live so far away, she doesn't get to spend nearly as much time with them as she does with my brothers and me.

"Good," I said. I found the courage to remove the pillow from my face. "Aughh, the sun is *bright!*"

"That's because it's a beautiful day out," Mom said cheerfully. "Now get a move on."

Nannie was supposed to arrive early in the afternoon. After I'd eaten lunch, I decided to sit on the front steps and wait for her. Louie came with me. He took a nap with his head resting on my knees while I watched the street.

I spotted Nannie's car when it was still a couple of blocks away. Nannie's car is easy to pick out. It's a secondhand car that's about a hundred years old, and when she bought it last year, she had it painted pink.

"Pink!" my mother exclaimed when she heard the news. "For heaven's sake, why pink?"

"Why not?" Nannie had answered gaily. And then she had fastened a pink plastic flower to the antenna and hung a little stuffed koala bear from the rearview mirror. She named her car the Pink Clinker. (It's not in very good condition.)

As the Pink Clinker pulled into our driveway, I woke Louie up, moved his head off my lap, and ran out to meet Nannie.

"Hi!" I called.

"Hi, there!" Nannie replied. She waved to me with one hand, and turned off the ignition with the other. The Pink Clinker shuddered into silence.

I helped Nannie into the house. She never comes over empty-handed. She carried a casserole, and I carried her pocketbook, a shopping bag full of presents, and her recipe box. (Mom and Nannie were going to discuss hors d'oeuvres or something.)

When Nannie had had a chance to sit down with a cup of tea on the back porch, I asked her an urgent question. "How's my dress coming?"

"Now, Kristy, don't pester Nannie," said Mom as she and David Michael joined us on the porch.

"Oh, she's not pestering me," said Nannie with a smile. "She's just excited. Kristy, your dress is coming along nicely. But I think the sleeves are going to be a bit long, so I want to measure your arms again."

"How much is done?"

"Well, it's almost all basted together," Nannie answered. "Karen's dress, too. But they're both a long way from being finished."

"Oh." My face fell.

"But don't worry. They'll be ready by Saturday. I promise."

"Okay," I said uncertainly, even though Nannie has never broken a promise.

"Kristy, relax," said Mom. "Have a cup of tea with us. Then I want you to round up your brothers so you kids can give me a hand with some things."

"Some things" turned out to be cleaning the entire house. Mom handed Charlie the floor waxer, Sam the vacuum cleaner, me a roll of paper towels and a bottle of Windex, and David Michael a rag and a can of furniture polish. Then she and Nannie holed up in the kitchen and talked about wedding food.

It was not as if wedding food hadn't already been discussed endlessly, but Mom and Nannie had to figure out how to instruct seven adults to prepare hundreds of hors d'oeuvres (appetizers) and canapés (crackers with stuff on them), not to mention salads and desserts, during the week. Mom had been very lucky in finding a caterer who, on short notice, could prepare the main dish for the buffet at the reception, but she and Watson were on their own for everything else.

By late afternoon, the house was shiny and clean, Mom and Nannie were through with recipes for the time being, and the relatives were arriving. The first were Aunt Theo (Mom's younger sister), and Uncle Neal, with Emma, Beth, and Luke.

They drove up, honking.

"They're here! They're here!" David Michael called, and all of us, including Nannie, dashed outside.

Uncle Neal was just getting out of the car. He is not my favorite relative. His pants and shirt never match, he smokes cigars, and he talks too loudly. But he's really okay. At least he never says to me, "My, Kristy, how you've grown. What grade are you in now?"

That's Aunt Theo's department. She stepped lightly out of the car and began hugging everyone. The second she got to me, she said, "My, Kristy, how you've grown. What grade are you in?"

"I'll be in eighth," I replied, and thought, And I have *not* grown. I'm the shortest person in my grade.

She moved on to David Michael. "My, how you've grown," she told him. "What grade are you in?"

I stood behind Aunt Theo and crossed my eyes at David Michael. He tried not to laugh as he replied, "Second."

During all this, Luke and Emma had scrambled out of the car. I took a good look at them, since I hadn't seen them in almost two years.

Luke was the oldest, the oldest of all the kids we'd be sitting for, in fact. He seemed kind of skinny and little for ten (I should talk) and stood back shyly while his mother hugged everyone, his father told loud jokes, Mom and Nannie laughed, and Louie jumped up and down with doggie joy. Luke had a thatch of thick, dark-blond hair that quite possibly hadn't been brushed since December, and serious brown eyes.

Emma seemed to be the opposite of Luke. Although she looked like him — a little peanut of a thing, with messy blond ponytails and sparkling brown eyes — she raced around the yard excitedly.

"Hi, Nannie!" she cried. "Guess what, I won a second-place ribbon in the gymnastics meet! Did you bring me a present?"

Before Nannie had a chance to answer, Emma had rushed over to David Michael. "You're David Michael, right? I'm a year older than you are." She ran on to Louie, leaving my brother looking bewildered.

Uh-oh, I thought. Luke will probably be easy to baby-sit for, but Emma looks like a bundle of energy. I was glad she and Karen weren't going to be in the same group.

Suddenly I realized that little Beth was still sitting patiently in her car seat. I leaned into the car and said quietly, "Hi, there, Beth."

She regarded me solemnly. Didn't laugh, didn't cry. I figured she was sizing me up, so I decided not to push things. I sat down next to her. She was barefoot, and after a while I tickled her toes. Very slowly, a smile spread across her face until she was grinning.

"Want to get out of the car?" I asked her.

I unfastened about a million straps and buckles. Then Beth raised her arms and I picked her up. "Ooof, you're heavy!" I exclaimed.

"Mm-po-po?" she asked me.

"Whatever." Mary Anne would have to learn Beth's baby talk. I handed Beth to Aunt Theo, who looked surprised. "Goodness," she said, "I'm amazed that she let you pick her up. Ordinarily, she screams when a stranger comes too near her. We have the most awful time with baby-sitters."

At that moment, Sam caught my eye. He gave me a look that clearly said, "The Baby-sitters Club is really going to *earn* the six hundred dollars."

I stuck my tongue out at him.

*"Beep-beep! Beep-beep!"*

Another honking car was pulling into our driveway.

"Aunt Colleen! Uncle Wallace!" I shouted.

As soon as my aunt had opened her door and straightened up, I practically threw myself at her.

Colleen is my mom's youngest sister of all, the baby of the family. And I love her. She's sort of a younger version of Nannie — busy and active with a wild streak in her. She understands me so well, it's almost scary.

"Hi, punkin. How are you doing?" she asked. She held me tight for a few seconds.

"Fine," I answered. I drew away and she cupped my chin in her hand and looked at me critically.

Meanwhile, cousins were spilling out of the car. First came Berk, the six-year-old. He made a beeline for David Michael. We see the Millers more often than the Meiners, and David Michael and Berk are good pals. I was glad that I remembered to assign them to the same baby-sitting group.

David Michael and Berk, followed by Louie, ran off toward the back of the house.

Next out of the car was Peter, who's three. He climbed out slowly, with tears in his eyes.

"Hey, Peter," I said. "What's wrong?"

Peter snuffled miserably.

"He's a little carsick," Aunt Colleen answered for him.

"Yeah," said Grace, the five-year-old, jumping to the ground, "He just puked. All over his coloring book!" She looked gleeful.

"Grace, that's enough," said her mother.

"How do you feel now, Peter?" I asked nervously. He looked awfully green.

"Not too good," he replied.

"I better get him in the house," said Aunt Colleen.

I watched them run inside, then turned back to the car and realized that Ashley was still sitting in it and Uncle Wallace was leaning a pair of crutches next to her door.

"Ashley!" I cried. "What happened to you?"

"I broke my leg roller-skating."

"We didn't say anything," my uncle added, "because we didn't want anyone to think we shouldn't come. Old Ash here is actually in pretty good shape. You should see her zip around on her crutches."

"I'm almost as fast as I was on my skates!" she exclaimed.

I helped Uncle Wallace get Ashley out of the car, and she swung herself up our driveway and into the house. (She *was* fast.)

Nannie made a big fuss over Ashley, then gathered her grandchildren around her and handed out gifts. She even had presents for my brothers and me, although she sees us often and has plenty of opportunities to give us things. I guess she didn't want us to feel left out.

All of Nannie's presents were handmade. Mine was a beautiful sweater, bright red with little black Scottie dogs trotting across the front. I hugged Nannie and thanked her eight times.

After the presents, we ate supper on picnic tables in the backyard.

Here's what happened during the meal:

Beth stored up a cheekful of carrots as her father fed her, then spit them all over his shirt.

Peter and Grace got into a fight and began to cry.

Berk and David Michael got into a fight and began to cry.

Emma teased Ashley. Ashley whacked Emma with her crutch. Emma cried. Ashley was sent to the Millers' car and Emma was sent to the Meiners' car until they were ready to apologize to each other.

Luke did not say one word from the beginning of the meal to the end.

A horrible, stuffy feeling began to build up in my stomach. It might have been due to the big dinner I'd eaten. Or it might have been due to seeing the trouble caused by eight children with ten adults present.

What would the next day be like — with just five baby-sitters in charge of *fourteen* children?

## CHAPTER 7

*Wedding Countdown:*
*Monday — five days to go*

Stacey, Mary Anne, Dawn, and Claudia showed up at my house at eight-thirty sharp. Stacey brought her Kid-Kit, a box of games and toys she sometimes takes on baby-sitting jobs (we each have one); Dawn brought a big book of rhymes, songs, games, and activities for children; Mary Anne brought the club record book and notebook; and Claudia brought the nametags and some art supplies.

"Let's put on our own tags before we forget them," I said. "Then we better get organized."

"It's such a beautiful day," said Stacey as she slipped the red star over her head. "Maybe we should try to stay out in your backyard as much as possible, Kristy. The picnic tables

70

would be good for reading stories and coloring and stuff. And the kids can play ball, run after Louie, play games, anything — all in one place where we can easily keep an eye on them."

"Okay," I agreed. "We'll see how it goes. If it gets crazy, we can start splitting the groups up. Oh, Mary Anne, Mom got out our old playpen. You might need it."

"Thanks. That's perfect. I'll set it up outside so Tony and Beth can be with the big kids."

We set to work in the backyard.

Just before nine o'clock, the Millers arrived. While Mom talked to Aunt Colleen and Uncle Wallace, the members of the Baby-sitters Club showed Ashley, Berk, Grace, and Peter to the yard. We gave them their nametags, and I tried to introduce the kids to my friends and explain about the groups and leaders. But before I had gotten very far, Aunt Colleen called me from the back porch.

"Just a few instructions," she said, as I ran to her. "I know you and your friends will have your hands full today, but I need to tell you a couple of things. Peter goes down for a nap sometime after lunch — around two. Grace generally doesn't take a nap, but if she's cranky, she'll sometimes go down with Peter."

"Wait, I better write this down," I said.

I got a pencil and a pad of paper from the kitchen. "Okay, Peter — nap at two," I said to Aunt Colleen, trying to sound professional. "Grace — maybe a nap at two."

"Right," said my aunt.

Then she handed me two bottles of pills. "These are prescriptions," she told me. "Put them somewhere safe, out of reach of Peter and Beth and all the small children. I hope you won't need them, but you might. This bottle, the one with the pink cap, is Berk's. It's for his allergies. He's been in good shape lately, but if you're outdoors a lot and he starts wheezing, give him one of these and make sure he lies down inside for a while. He's used to this and knows what to do."

I scribbled away frantically. I was beginning to panic. What if Berk (or any of the children) got sick? One of us would have to care for the sick child, and the others would have to take over the rest of the kids from that group. Another thing: We hadn't thought to "childproof" my house. We were inviting little kids into a home where electric sockets, medicine, and poisonous cleaning supplies were all over the place. We didn't have to keep those things out of the way anymore. David Michael was seven years old and knew better. But when Aunt Colleen said to put the pills away in a safe place — where the little kids couldn't reach them — I began to worry.

However, my aunt didn't know what I was thinking. She was still talking. "These other pills," she was saying, "are painkillers. They're for Ashley. The doctor at the hospital gave them to us after he set her leg. Ashley hasn't taken one in a week, but every now and then her leg will swell under her cast, and it's quite painful. Give her *half* a pill with food if she complains of pain."

"Ashley — one half pill with food for pain," I repeated.

"I guess that's everything," said Aunt Colleen. "I don't think you'll have any problems."

"Great," I said. I took my notes outdoors so i could share them with the other members of the Baby-sitters Club.

So far, things in the backyard looked peaceful. Everyone was wearing a nametag (although Ashley was complaining that hers looked babyish), and the kids were exploring the yard and the toys in the Kid-Kit.

"Yoo-hoo! Kristy! We're he-ere!" It was Aunt Theo. (Who else would say, "Yoo-hoo"?)

"Hi!" I shouted.

Emma burst outside, followed, at a much slower pace, by Luke. Aunt Theo came last with Beth — and a lot of equipment.

"Hi, girls," said my aunt.

"Aunt Theo, this is Mary Anne, Stacey — "

"Fine, fine," my aunt interrupted. "Now I've brought Beth's Walk-a-Tot chair so she can scoot around safely. She loves the chair. And here's her stroller in case you want to take a walk. If she cries when we leave — and she probably will — just put her in the stroller and walk her around. She'll calm down after a while."

I looked at Mary Anne, who was taking notes this time. My head was swimming. Naptime, pills, strollers, Walk-a-Tots. . . . What had we gotten ourselves into?

Aunt Theo wasn't finished yet. "Beth usually takes two naps, one around eleven and another around two."

Well, that was something, I thought. At least the afternoon nappers would be asleep at the same time.

"And she usually takes a bottle to bed with her. Make sure you only give her the prepared bottles I brought. She's allergic to cow's milk, so the bottles are filled with a soy formula."

"Beth — allergic to milk," Mary Anne murmured.

I nudged Stacey. "Where are all these kids going to sleep?" I whispered.

Stacey widened her eyes. I guess she hadn't thought about naps and bottles and pills, either.

Aunt Theo finally stopped talking.

And just in time. Mary Anne, Stacey, Dawn, Claudia and I were about to get our first glimpse of the Fielding kids. Mom was leading a whole passel of people into the backyard — all six Fieldings, plus Watson, Andrew, and Karen.

Courage, I told myself. Make like you're the Cowardly Lion. If you *think* you're courageous, then you'll *be* courageous.

"Honey," Mom said to me, "I want you to meet Mr. and Mrs. Fielding."

I shook their hands. Then I said, "And these are the other members of the Baby-sitters Club — Stacey, Dawn, Mary Anne, and Claudia."

Everyone exchanged hellos.

Karen took Andrew's hand and led him to the table where Claudia's art stuff was set out. "I'm going to draw a big, ugly picture of Morbidda Destiny," I could hear her say.

But the Fieldings hadn't moved an inch. A baby was huddled in his mother's arms with his face buried in her neck. A girl about Grace's age was holding Mr. Fielding's hand solemnly.

And a little boy and girl were clutching their father around his legs, their faces also buried.

Watson leaned over and whispered to me, "They're all very shy."

Now this is the sort of thing that kills me about Watson. Duh. Of course they were shy. Any fool could see that.

Mrs. Fielding spoke quietly to her children. "This is where you're going to play today. Andrew and Karen are here. See?" She pointed to the table where Andrew and Karen were coloring and giggling.

I knelt down to child level. "I'm Kristy. We're going to have lots of fun," I said. "There are swings and games and friends to play with."

The oldest child (Katherine?) bit her lip and gripped her mother's hand more tightly.

"Do you like dogs?" I tried. "We've got old Louie — "

"A dog, Daddy?" whimpered the little boy.

Oops, bad idea, I thought.

Mrs. Fielding tried to untwine the baby from around her neck. "This is Tony," she said. "I think I'll just put him in the playpen."

She did so, with Katherine trailing behind, holding onto her mother's jeans skirt.

Tony's face slowly crumbled. He sat on his bottom with his arms in the air and his lower lip trembling. His eyes filled with tears. Then, very slowly, he opened his mouth and let out a shrill, "Wahh!!"

Mary Anne turned pale.

Mrs. Fielding looked flustered. "I think — well, we'll just leave him there. He'll stop crying after a while. Now, this is Katherine."

"And this," said Mr. Fielding, indicating the little boy attached to his left leg, "is Patrick. And this is Maura." (Little girl attached to right leg.)

Katherine, Patrick, and Maura made no moves to leave their parents.

I glanced at Mom. Mom glanced at Watson. They talked to each other with their eyes. Finally Watson clapped his hands together and said heartily, "Are the adults ready to go?"

"We have a lot to do today," added my mother.

Mr. Fielding pulled Patrick and Maura off his legs.

Mrs. Fielding got herself out of Katherine's grip. "We'll see you this afternoon," she said to her children. I could tell that Mr. and Mrs. Fielding were having as much trouble leaving as their children were having letting them go.

The adults walked around to the front of the house and piled into their cars.

Katherine, Patrick, Maura, Tony, Beth, and

Peter all began to cry. Andrew took stock of the situation and began to cry, too.

Something else us baby-sitters didn't count on: seven crying children.

"Quick, put on the rest of the nametags and divide into groups," I said.

We did. Stacey and Dawn had no criers, Mary Anne and I had two criers each, and every kid in Claudia's group was crying.

But nobody panicked. Mary Anne put Tony in Beth's Walk-a-Tot and Beth in her stroller, and walked Beth around the yard as Aunt Theo had suggested.

I talked quietly to Andrew and he stopped crying right away. After all, he knew where he was. Then I took my group off to a corner of the yard, pulled Katherine onto my lap, and began to read *Green Eggs and Ham*.

Claudia had a tougher job, but she did what I did, and led her three criers to a different corner, sat down and began reading *Where the Sidewalk Ends.* Soon every one of our criers had become a giggler. And Mary Anne's criers were quiet.

When I finished reading *Green Eggs and Ham*, I looked around the yard and took a fast head count. Stacey was sitting at one of the picnic tables with Luke, Ashley, and Emma. They were making woven placemats out of construction paper.

Nearby, Dawn was playing monkey-in-the-middle with David Michael, Berk, and Karen.

Claudia and I were reading to our groups, and Mary Anne had successfully put both babies in the playpen and was tickling their feet.

Good. Fourteen happy children. The first crisis was over.

The rest of the morning went fairly smoothly. There were a few arguments and tears, but nothing to complain about. At lunchtime, we seated the twelve older children around the picnic tables, and put Tony in the Walk-a-Tot and Beth in her stroller. Then Stacey and Dawn went into the kitchen to get the children's lunches. Mom had asked the parents to pack a separate lunch for each kid. This was a little hard on my aunts and uncles since they were staying in a motel, but it worked well because my friends and I didn't have to spend time making lunch. Also, we knew the parents would send food their kids would eat. This was important: We had a lot of picky eaters and a few kids with food allergies.

After lunch Tony, Beth, Maura, Patrick, and

Peter went down for naps. We simply lined them up on a blanket in the living room, and after a while they all fell asleep.

Good timing. At two-thirty a horn beeped in our driveway.

"That's Nannie," I told Mary Anne. "She's here for Karen and me."

Nannie was helping out at Watson's that week, too, and she was supposed to take Karen and me to the florist to look at wedding flowers. Mary Anne was watching the nappers while Claudia took over my group. Claudia was reading to Grace, Katherine, and Andrew on a blanket under a tree, and the three of them looked pretty drowsy.

"Come on, Karen!" I called.

Karen raced across the yard and we scrambled into the Pink Clinker.

"How come we're going to see the flower lady, Nannie?" Karen asked. (Nannie isn't any relation to Karen, of course, but Karen loves my grandmother and started calling her Nannie the first time they met.)

"We have to see about flowers for your hair," Nannie told her.

"Flowers for my hair?" Karen squealed with delight.

"And for Kristy's," said Nannie. "You two will have matching flowers."

"What about the flowers for my basket?" Karen wanted to know.

"Rose petals. We'll talk to the florist about them, too. And Kristy, we'll see about your bouquet."

Who would have thought that choosing a few flowers could be so difficult? You would have thought we were choosing flowers for a royal wedding in London instead of just Mom and Watson's backyard wedding.

First, Nannie showed the woman in the store swatches of the material from Karen's dress and my gown, which were going to be yellow. The woman said, "How about white flowers?" and Karen said, "Yuck," and Nannie said, "Salmon," and I said, "Yuck," and Karen said, "What's salmon?" and I said, "It's a fish," and Karen said, "Yuck" again.

After about fifteen minutes of that, we finally settled on yellow and white, with yellow petals for Karen's basket.

But the job was only half done. We still had to decide how Karen and I would wear our hair so the florist would know whether to make up wreaths or rosettes or what.

An hour later, we left. I was exhausted.

And a herd of children would be waiting for me when I got home.

However, coming home turned out to be the nicest part of the day. The little kids were rested from their naps and stories, and the older kids were excited because Stacey and Dawn had helped them put together a play, which they performed with great delight for Claudia, Mary Anne, me, and the younger children.

At five o'clock, the parents came home to fourteen happy children.

The members of the Baby-sitters Club decided that the first day had been a success.

## CHAPTER 8

Wedding Countdown:
Tuesday — four days to go

Tuesday, June 23rd

Today was another bright, sunny day, thank goodness, and almost as warm as a nice September day in California. Yesterday was fine with all the kids in Kristy's back yard, but we decided to do different things this morning. The kids would get tired of the Thomases' yard pretty quickly. So after the parents left, Mary Anne took the babies for a walk, Stacey took the red group to the brook to catch minnows, Kristy and Claudia walked their groups to the public library for story hour, and I took David Michael, Berk, and Karen to the school playground.

What a morning my group had— all thanks to Karen's imagination.

Tuesday morning started off a lot like Monday morning, except that the mothers didn't have any more instructions, us baby-sitters were a lot more confident and a lot less worried, and Mr. Fielding had a much easier time prying Maura and Patrick off his legs.

When the parents left, there were only six criers (Andrew barely noticed that Watson was gone), and they were just crying token cries, except for the babies, who kept Mary Anne's hands full for quite a while.

We had agreed the evening before that we would take the kids on the trips that Dawn described in the Baby-sitters Club Notebook, and we decided to get started right away.

We must have looked pretty funny.

First of all, once the pink group had calmed down, Mary Anne had to fit both babies into Beth's stroller. It wasn't easy, but finally she sort of smushed Tony into Beth's lap.

Claudia and I had to get seven small children (our two groups, plus Jamie Newton) all the way to the library. We figured it would take about half an hour to walk them there.

"Wagons!" said Claudia suddenly.

"Oh, great idea!" I breathed a sigh of relief. Then I loaded Maura, Patrick, and Peter into

David Michael's old wagon, and Claudia loaded Grace, Katherine, and Andrew into Mary Anne's old wagon. After we each packed a bag containing graham crackers, cans of juice, toys, extra diapers, and spare training pants, we were ready to pick up Jamie and go.

Despite the fact that David Michael hadn't used his wagon in at least two years, he yelled after me as I pulled my load down the driveway, "And those kids better not hurt my wagon while you're gone, Kristy!"

It must be a little hard for him practically to have a day-care center in his house.

Anyway, everyone left for wherever they were going. Stacey set off for the brook with Luke, Ashley, and Emma. They reached it pretty quickly, even with Ashley gallumping along on her crutches, and settled in for a morning of fun, which Stacey told me about later.

Stacey had brought along a garbage bag to wrap around Ashley's cast so it wouldn't get wet. Even so, Ashley wasn't able to do much at first.

"I can't get into a good fishing position!" she exclaimed. "My leg just won't go that way."

It was true. Luke and Emma were crouching

along the bank with pails and nets, but Ashley could only stand up or sit with her leg straight in front of her.

"I could help you wade," Stacey said uncertainly. "You could take off your sneaker, and I could help you stand in the brook on your good leg."

Ashley looked from her cast to the water tumbling over the rocks and then at Stacey. "I better not," she said, sounding disappointed.

"It's probably just as well," replied Stacey. But she was afraid Ashley would be bored.

It turned out that she didn't have to worry. Ashley sat down a safe distance from the bank and assigned herself all sorts of jobs, like minnow-counter and storyteller. Later, she moved to a patch of clover and made clover jewelry for the whole group.

Meanwhile, Mary Anne was walking the babies. The arrangement in the stroller had lasted about two minutes. Then Beth wanted to get out and walk. At first that seemed like a good solution, but Beth wasn't very steady on her feet yet, and toddled along slowly, often losing her balance and sitting down on the sidewalk. After ten minutes, they had traveled about six feet.

Thanks to the wagons, Claudia and I were

having somewhat better luck, even though every few seconds one of us would have to turn around and call out, "Keep your hands in the wagon!" or, "Don't dangle your feet over the side!"

On the way to the library, we stopped at the Newtons' house.

"Hi-hi!" Jamie shouted when he saw us.

We introduced him to the other kids — and then realized there was no room for him to sit down. Three kids in a wagon was already a tight squeeze.

"Hey," said Claudia, "you know what we need? We need a wagon watcher. The wagon watcher walks beside the wagons. When he sees anybody sticking their hands and feet outside of the wagon, he gets to trade places with that person, and that person is the new wagon watcher."

Claudia's idea was great. None of the kids wanted to be caught by the wagon watcher, yet they all wanted a chance to *be* the wagon watcher (except for Maura, who was really too little to understand the game). So we rolled cheerfully to the library, stopping eight times to switch kids, and arrived exactly one minute before the start of story hour.

Now, while we were on our way to the

library, and Mary Anne was inching along with the pink group, and Stacey was taking Luke, Ashley, and Emma to the brook, Dawn was walking the three bluebirds to the elementary school playground. This might seem like an easy job, and in fact it started out that way, but Karen Brewer always seems to make things more interesting than usual.

Tuesday was no exception.

"You know what?" she said, as she, Dawn, David Michael, and Berk reached the end of our street.

"What?" asked David Michael warily. He had heard enough stories about witches and ghosts from Karen to be suspicious whenever she said, "You know what?"

"Yesterday when I got home, this big kid on my street said that at seven o'clock tonight, an army of Martians is going to attack the earth."

"Martians?" yelped David Michael.

"Tonight?" cried Berk.

"That's just a story, a joke," Dawn told them.

"No, it's true," Karen insisted. "This was a *big* kid. He's in *eighth grade.* He told me that a lot of people know about this, but they just don't want to believe it. Only the ones who believe will be safe, because they'll be able to hide in time."

"Hide where?" asked Berk.

"Underground," said Karen.

"In a hole?" said David Michael.

"I'm not sure," replied Karen slowly. "The kid didn't say."

"Karen, you know this is all just silly stuff, don't you?" asked Dawn.

"*No,*" said Karen firmly. "No way. This is not silly stuff."

"There are no such things as Martians," Dawn told Berk and David Michael.

David Michael looked like he wanted to believe her, but he said, "I've seen Martians on TV."

Dawn noticed then that all three kids kept glancing up at the sky.

"Do you believe everything you see on TV?" asked Dawn. "Do you believe that Bugs Bunny and Mickey Mouse are real?"

"No," said David Michael, "but there might be Martians."

"Yeah," agreed Berk. "There might be Martians."

"There are no Martians," Dawn repeated, exasperated.

"Are, too," said David Michael, Karen, and Berk at the same time.

"I wonder what will happen," my brother went on quietly.

"You wonder what will happen when?" Dawn asked him.

"When they land."

Dawn threw her hands in the air. There was no point in arguing.

"They're going to fight us," Karen said fiercely.

"Martians have ray guns," Berk added. "Ray guns and spray guns."

"Spray guns?" repeated David Michael, alarmed.

"Yeah. They spray stuff on you so you can't move. Then they just pick you up and put you in their flying saucer and speed you away to Mars."

"Are they coming in flying saucers tonight, Karen?" asked David Michael.

"Hundreds of 'em," Karen answered. "All shiny and silvery."

David Michael searched the sky so long that he tripped and fell on his knees. "I thought I saw one!" he said breathlessly as he stood up. "Now it's gone."

They had almost reached the playground. Dawn tried to distract her group. "Hey, look at this!" she said, pointing to a poster that was tacked to the fence surrounding the school-yard. " 'Arts and crafts today. Puppet-making contest.' A contest, you guys! Wouldn't you like to enter? I wonder what the prize is. . . . You guys?"

"Huh?" The three bluebirds were looking at the sky.

"I wonder if you could hide in your basement," David Michael whispered. "That's underground."

"Can I stay at your house tonight?" Berk asked my brother. "I don't know if the motel has a basement."

*"Berk!"* Dawn cried. "David Michael! Karen! *Enough!"* She thought about telling them they weren't allowed to discuss Martians anymore, but decided that was too mean.

She led them through the gate and into the playground.

A handful of children were playing on the swings and seesaws and monkey bars. A big group was seated around a table that was covered with paints, scraps of felt, glue, scissors, buttons, and all sorts of trimmings.

"How about making puppets?" Dawn suggested desperately. "Let's at least find out what the prize is."

The three kids looked at each other. Karen leaned over and whispered something to David Michael and Berk.

"Hey, no secrets!" said Dawn. Karen finished whispering and the boys nodded their heads.

"We'd rather swing," said Karen.

"All right," Dawn agreed uncertainly. "You go ahead. I'm going to see about the contest."

Dawn found the playground counselor at the arts and crafts table. She asked her about the contest and about what other activities were coming up. She thought Stacey might want to bring Emma, Luke, and Ashley to the playground later in the week.

Their conversation was interrupted by an ear-piercing shriek. Dawn whirled around, afraid one of the bluebirds was hurt. Instead, a little girl came tearing across the playground and threw herself at the counselor.

"Fran! Fran!" she cried.

"Tina, what's wrong?" The counselor picked Tina up and gave her a hug.

"Martians!" Tina managed to sob.

Uh-oh, thought Dawn.

"Martians!" exclaimed Fran. "What do you mean, honey?"

"They're coming! Tonight! They're going to take us away!"

That was all Dawn needed to hear. She turned around and marched across the schoolyard. Karen and my brother and cousin were at the swings, all right, but they weren't swinging. They were surrounded by an awed bunch of kids.

Dawn reached them in time to hear Karen saying, ". . . hide underground."

"Like in your basement," David Michael added.

The other children were looking at them with fear in their eyes. One boy was wiping tears away. Suddenly, he turned and ran.

"Where are you going?" another boy shouted after him.

"Home!"

"I'm coming with you!"

"Me, too!" chorused the others. The entire group fled toward the gate to the playground.

"Karen Brewer . . ." Dawn warned.

Karen looked up guiltily. "Yeah?"

"I do *not* want you scaring the other kids with that story."

"But we have to *warn* them. They have to be ready for the attack." Karen was quite serious about that.

"Right," said Berk and David Michael.

"Wrong," said Dawn. "Now come over to the arts and crafts table and forget about the Martians."

Dawn settled her charges with Fran and the other kids. They began to work busily. She was helping Berk put a nose on his puppet when she heard a crashing noise behind her. She looked around and saw a branch falling from a tree nearby.

"Martians!" Karen screamed.

"Aughh!" shrieked David Michael and Berk.

"I want my mommy!" cried Tina.

"Martians?" asked several children.

"Coming to get us!" Karen told them. "They're going to attack! They're here already! We have to hide!"

Every single child at the art table scrambled out of his or her seat and rushed for cover.

Fran turned to Dawn, looking slightly cross.

"I'm sorry," Dawn said quickly. "I don't know what got into her. I'll take her home as soon as I help you find the kids."

"That's all right," said Fran. "Another counselor will be here in about ten minutes. He can help me. Please take her home now, okay?"

"Okay." Dawn paused, then added, "I really am sorry."

Fran nodded.

"Karen Brewer!" Dawn called. "Berk! David Michael. I want you three to come out right this minute. Do you hear me?"

Nothing.

"There are *no Martians*," Dawn added. "Just me. And I'm getting mad."

The blue group crawled sheepishly out of a storage shed.

"Come on," said Dawn. "We have to leave." She wondered if she should tell Karen to apologize to Fran, but Fran looked busy and annoyed. Dawn hustled the three kids away.

As they walked home, she gave them a talk about telling stories and scaring children, and Karen became grave and concerned. She promised not to mention the Martians again. David Michael and Berk promised, too.

The bluebirds were the first group to return to my house that day, even beating Mary Anne and the babies. They were on their best behavior all afternoon, and Tuesday passed quickly.

Late that night, after my lights were out and I was in bed, something occurred to me. Wedding presents were starting to arrive at our house. The wedding was then just about three days away. I would have to get a present for Mom and Watson, but what? What do you get for your mother and a millionaire? They already had everything they needed and could buy anything they wanted.

I lay awake thinking. My present had to be just right.

# CHAPTER 9

*Wedding Countdown:*
*Wednesday — three days to go*

Wednesday, June 24th

This is a confession, you guys. I know you think I'm so sophisticated, since I'm from New York and my hair is permed and everything, but no kidding, my favorite movie is "Mary Poppins." I've seen it 65 times. (That's because we bought the movie so that I could watch it on the VCR whenever I want, and I watch it at least once a week.) I know it by heart. Anyway, when I saw that it was going to be at the Embassy Theater for a "special engagement", I decided I had to have another chance to see it on a big screen. That's one reason I was so determined to take the red group to it. Besides, since it's my favorite movie, I was sure Luke, Emma, and Ashley would love it, too. Believe me, if I'd had a crystal ball to see into the future, I would never have taken them.

Stacey didn't mention it in her notebook entry, but one o'clock on Wednesday marked the halfway point of the Baby-sitters Club's adventure taking care of fourteen children. Two and a half days were behind us. Two and a half days were ahead of us.

Of course, we'd had our share of problems.

There was Dawn's experience at the playground, for instance. "I keep thinking of all those scared children," she said. "Especially the ones who ran home. I hope they found mommies or daddies or big brothers or sisters who told them not to worry. And Karen can't ever show up at that playground again, at least not as long as Fran is the counselor."

Then there was the problem with bathrooms. We have three: one downstairs and two upstairs. One of the upstairs ones is Mom's and off limits, which left two bathrooms for nineteen people, two of whom were in diapers and needed to be changed a lot, and one of whom (Maura) had only recently been potty-trained.

It seemed as if somebody always had to use the bathroom. Since the little kids were more urgent about it ("Kristy, Kristy! I have to go *now!*"), we decided that the yellow group, green group, and pink group would use the downstairs bathroom, which was nearer; and the five baby-sitters, the red group, and the blue group would use the upstairs bathroom. We stuck a yellow sun, a green dinosaur, and a pink heart on the door of the first-floor bathroom, and a red star and a bluebird on the door of the second-floor bathroom as reminders. But there were always mix-ups.

"Kristy, which bathroom do I use?" David Michael asked me as I was rummaging through the refrigerator, getting the lunches out on Wednesday.

"What group are you in?"

"I don't know."

"Well, look at your nametag," I told him.

"I lost it."

"You're a bluebird. Go upstairs."

"I was just up there. Somebody's in it."

"Then wait."

"I can't."

"Then go downstairs."

"Someone's in there, too."

"David Michael, you're going to have to wait, or else go across the street and ask Mimi to let you use the Kishis' bathroom."

"No way!"

At that moment, Luke and Andrew walked out of the house and into the backyard.

"I think the bathrooms are free," I said.

"*Which* one do I use?"

I groaned. "It doesn't matter. Just go."

The kids had almost as much trouble keeping their groups straight. The baby-sitters knew who their charges were, but even with the nametags, the kids were never sure. If Stacey, for instance, called for the red group, eight children would run to her.

But none of that mattered much. As long as we could be outside, we were fine. The kids were having fun.

Wednesday afternoon was the special showing of *Mary Poppins*. Stacey had known about it for several days, and on Tuesday she asked my aunts and uncles for permission to take the red group to the Embassy and for money to buy tickets.

The Embassy was all the way downtown, but Nannie was going to take me shoe shopping that afternoon (while Mary Anne watched the nappers again), so she planned to drop Stacey and the red group at the theater on our way to the mall, and pick them up on our way back.

The Pink Clinker was loaded down as Nannie pulled out of the driveway. "I'll drive very slowly," she told Ashley, who was sitting next to her in the front seat. "I don't want to jar your leg."

"I hope she doesn't drive *too* slowly," Stacey whispered to me. "I don't want to miss the beginning."

Nannie did creep along, but we reached the theater in plenty of time for the show.

Luke and Emma hopped out of the car, while Stacey helped Ashley out.

"Good-bye!" Nannie called as the Pink Clinker roared to life. "Have fun! I'll be back in two hours."

Stacey led the three kids to the ticket window. "Now, do you all have your money?" she asked.

"Yup," said Luke.

"Yup," said Ashley.

"Nope," said Emma.

*"Nope?"* Stacey repeated. "Emma, where is it? I told you three kids to make sure you brought your money."

"I *did* bring it," Emma whined.

"Mine's in my pocket," said Luke.

"Mine's in my knapsack," said Ashley.

Emma looked blank. "I don't *know* where mine is."

"I'd pay for you," Stacey told her, "but I've only got about a dollar extra. Emma, think. What did you do with your money?"

"I don't *kno-ow*." (She was a good whiner. Very good.)

"Do want me to call Kristy's house and see if you left it there by mistake? Maybe Claudia's grandmother could drive it over here," she said uncertainly.

"All right," agreed Emma, scuffing the toe of her sneaker along the sidewalk.

"Stacey, I'm going to sit down on that bench," said Ashley.

"Okay. This'll only take a sec. I hope." Stacey fished a quarter out of the pocket of her overalls and called my house.

Mary Anne answered the phone.

Stacey could hear crying in the background. "What's going on?" she asked.

"The phone woke the babies."

"Oops."

"What's up? I thought you were at the movies."

"We're almost there. Emma can't find her money. She thinks she might have left it at Kristy's. . . . Would you mind looking?"

"Well, no. Let me just quiet Tony and Beth down. Then I'll look around. Hold on."

Mary Anne looked so long that Stacey's quarter ran out and the pay phone clicked off.

"Darn!" exclaimed Stacey. She didn't have much change left. She put a dime and three nickels in the slot and called back.

The line was busy. It was still off the hook.

Stacey was growing impatient. The movie would start in five minutes. She tried again.

"Stacey?" said Mary Anne. "Where were you?"

"We got cut off. Did you find the money?"

"No, and I looked everywhere. Dawn and Claudia looked, too."

"Oh, brother. This is great, just great."

Emma was tugging on Stacey's sleeve. "Stacey?" she asked.

"Just a minute," Stacey told her.

"Stacey, it's important."

"Not now, Emma."

"But Stacey, I found my money."

Stacey looked at Emma, who was holding her money out triumphantly. "Mary Anne?" she said. "Never mind. We found it."

Stacey thanked Mary Anne and hung up. "Where was it?" she asked Emma.

"In my shoe."

Stacey shook her head. "Well, hurry up, you guys. The movie's starting."

She helped Ashley over to the ticket window. Then, to save time, she collected the money from her group, gave it all to the man in the booth, and said, "One adult and three children, please."

The man handed four tickets to Stacey, who in turn handed them to a young woman at the entrance to the lobby, while Emma, Luke, and Ashley filed in ahead of her.

"Go right into the theater. Hurry, you guys," said Stacey. "The lights are about to. . . ."

But the kids weren't listening to her. They were standing at the candy counter, looking like they hadn't eaten in weeks.

"I want Junior Mints," said Emma.

"I want M&M's," said Luke.

"I want popcorn," said Ashley.

"We don't have enough time — or money," Stacey said. She glanced into the theater. The lights were dimming. "Besides, you just ate lunch."

"But we have room for a snack," said Emma, who was on the verge of whining again. "And our moms gave us extra money for a movie treat."

It took five minutes to buy the candy and popcorn. When the children were ready, they tiptoed into the dark theater.

"We need four seats together, with one on the aisle for Ashley," Stacey whispered loudly to them.

"*Shh!*" said a woman nearby.

They walked up and down the aisles. Finally an usher with a flashlight found seats for them in the balcony.

Toward the end of the movie, Emma spilled

the last of her sticky Junior Mints over the railing. Below her, someone shrieked. Emma began to giggle and couldn't stop. Ashley began to giggle, too, and after a while even Luke joined in.

The usher ushered them outside.

Stacey stood on the sidewalk, her cheeks flaming, and was never so relieved as when she saw the Pink Clinker cruising down the street.

She climbed into the car, her eyes blazing.

"What happened?" I asked, not sure I really wanted to know.

"Ask *her*," Stacey said, glaring at Emma.

Emma tried to tell me, but she began giggling again. Before I knew it, Ashley and Luke were giggling, too.

Their laughter was contagious. Nannie and I caught it. When I dared to look at Stacey, I found that even she was laughing.

"Oh, well," she said as Nannie pulled into our driveway, "I can always see *Mary Poppins* on TV."

That was Wednesday. I now had my wedding shoes — low with a little heel — but no idea about a gift for Mom and Watson.

# CHAPTER 10

## Wedding Countdown:
## Thursday — two days to go

Thursday, June 25th

Until today, I didn't know that "barber" is a dirty word. But it is — to little boys. Here's how I found out: When the mothers and fathers dropped their children off at Kristy's house this morning, they all looked guilty. It turned out that they'd decided the boys, except for Tony, needed their hair cut before the wedding. Since the barber is only open from 9:00 until 5:00, guess what they asked us poor, defenseless, unprepared baby-sitters to do? They asked us to take Luke, David Michael, Berk, Andrew, Peter, and Patrick to poor, defenseless, unprepared Mr. Gates, whose barbershop is just around the corner from the elementary school. When we told the boys about their field trip, all six of them turned pale, then red, and began throwing tantrums...

Well, Mary Anne may not have been prepared for the trip to the barbershop, but I've gone there with David Michael many times, so I had a dim idea of what could happen. You just take David Michael's tears and whining and complaining and multiply them by six. That's what I thought. But there must have been something wrong with my calculations, because the boys definitely caused more than six times the trouble my brother causes by himself.

After the adults left that morning, the members of the Baby-sitters Club turned the children loose in the backyard and held a quick meeting on the porch while we kept an eye on things.

"Six boys will be going to Mr. Gates'," I said, "and the seven girls plus Tony will stay behind. How should we divide ourselves up? Should three of us go to the barber?"

"That sounds like too many," said Dawn. "Doesn't Mr. Gates have an assistant? Two boys can get their hair cut at once. Then there'll only be four to watch."

"That's true," I said. "Okay, two of us will go and three will stay here. I better be one of the ones to go, since I'm related to most of those boys."

Mary Anne giggled.

"Who else wants to go?" I could tell that the other baby-sitters wanted the easy job of staying at my house with the girls and Tony.

At last Mary Anne spoke up. "I'll go with you, Kristy," she said. "I've been stuck here with Beth and Tony all week."

"Are you sure you want to do this?" I asked her.

"Positive," she replied, sounding entirely unsure of herself.

"All right," I said just as uncertainly.

You've probably never taken a ten-year-old, a seven-year-old, a six-year-old, a four-year-old, and two three-year-olds to the barber. I certainly never had. Mary Anne and I waited until the kids had eaten lunch before we rounded the boys up. After lunch, the kids were full and the younger ones tended to be sleepy.

When the trash had been cleared away and the picnic tables wiped off, I stood bravely in the backyard and announced, "Okay, barber-time."

"No-no-no-no-no!" shrieked Andrew.

Peter and Patrick joined in. "No-no-no-no-no!"

Luke, David Michael, and Berk were too old for no-no's. They climbed a tree instead.

"We're not coming down!" David Michael shouted.

"Fine," I said. "Mary Anne, will you get Nannie on the phone, please, and tell her to bring the Pink Clinker over here? Tell her the boys are — "

"Wait! Wait! Here we come!" cried Berk. The boys jumped out of the tree.

Nannie is a terrific grandmother, but she expects kids to do what they're told, and when it's time for discipline, she is very firm about things.

"Thanks," I said to the older boys.

They didn't answer. David Michael scowled at me. At last he said, "You want me to look like an owl, don't you? That's what I looked like after I went to Mr. Gates the last time. An owl. A horned owl. My hair just got normal, and now you and Mom are going to make me look like an owl again."

"David Michael, for heaven's sake, calm down. After all, it's Mom's wedding. She wants you to look good. If she thought Mr. Gates was going to make you look like a horned owl, I'm sure she wouldn't send you to him."

"No barber," Peter spoke up piteously.

"Sorry, guys," I said. "Haircuts all around. Let's get going."

"I'll go find a wagon," Mary Anne offered. "Peter and Patrick and Andrew can ride in it."

As the boys filed out of the yard, the girls watched them.

Nobody said a word for the longest time. Finally, Emma couldn't stand it any longer.

"Ha, ha. Ha, ha. You guys — "

Ashley hobbled forward and clapped her hand over Emma's mouth.

Emma tried to bite her.

"*Ow!* Quit it!"

"Well, leave me alone!" exclaimed Emma.

Mary Anne whispered to me, "The girls may be harder to handle than the boys!"

We loaded the little guys into the wagon, and in no time were ushering the boys into Mr. Gates' place.

Now, if I'd been Mr. Gates and had seen six unhappy boys come in for haircuts, I might have had a nervous breakdown. But not Mr. Gates. He simply finished up the customer he was working on, then turned to Mary Anne and me. "Well, what have we here?" he asked pleasantly.

"Isn't it obvious?" murmured Luke.

Mary Anne shot Luke a hideous look and he quieted down.

I stepped forward. "Hi, Mr. Gates," I said. "My mom's getting married on Saturday — "

"Well, congratulations!"

"Thanks. And my brother's going to be *in* the wedding, and the rest of these guys are going to be *at* the wedding, and they all need their hair cut."

"But not too short," said David Michael.

"Not over my ears," said Luke.

"Not too long at the sides," said Berk.

"Leave my part alone," said Andrew.

"I don't *want* a part," said Peter.

"Do you have lollipops?" asked Patrick.

"One at a time, one at a time," said Mr. Gates calmly. "Do you know Mr. Pratt? He's the other barber here."

A skinny, jumpy-looking man stepped in from the back room, and right away I sensed trouble. He must have been new. I didn't remember seeing him before. He laughed nervously.

"Mr. Pratt," said Mr. Gates, "these young men need haircuts."

"All of them? Heh-heh."

"That's right." Mr. Gates turned back to the boys. "Okay, which two will be first?"

"Not me!" said six voices.

Mary Anne made a quick decision. "Luke and David Michael," she said. It was a good idea. They were the two oldest.

"No," said both boys.

I took them aside. "There's a phone in the corner," I told them, pointing to it. "And I've got change in my pocket. I can get hold of Nannie easily."

"Okay, okay," said Luke.

"David Michael, you go with Mr. Pratt. And be *good*."

Meanwhile, Mary Anne had taken the four younger boys to some chairs by the front door. She was trying to get them to sit down, but they were climbing over everything like monkeys.

"Come *on*," Mary Anne urged them.

"I'm Rocket Man!" cried Peter.

"Not in here you aren't." Mary Anne picked Peter up and sat him in her lap.

I didn't know whether to help her or to watch Luke and David Michael. I decided I better keep an eye on the boys, and especially on my brother and Mr. Pratt.

David Michael climbed into the barber chair as if he were on his way to a funeral.

"Well, heh-heh," said Mr. Pratt.

"Don't make me look like a horned owl," said David Michael rudely. He caught sight of me glaring at him in the mirror and stuck his tongue out.

Mr. Pratt thought it was meant for him.

"Oh, goodness, heh-heh." He patted his

pockets, searching for something, then walked into the back room.

Luke leaned over from the next chair and whispered to David Michael, "He probably forgot his brain."

"Now, now," said Mr. Gates. "Hmm. It seems to me I've got a box of lollipops over by the cash register. But I only give them to my well-behaved customers."

"I'm too old for lollipops," said Luke.

"Me, too," said David Michael, who had asked for two the last time he'd had his hair cut.

That did it.

"Excuse me a sec, Mr. Gates," I said. I stepped between the chairs and said to the boys, "You two are being plain rude. Who taught you to speak this way to adults? I can't believe it. I want you to know that I am now walking over to that phone and calling Nannie. I guess I just can't take care of you guys after all. My friends and I tried to make things fun for you, but you're too much to handle. I'll have to turn the job over to Nannie."

"No, Kristy! Please don't!" David Michael cried. "We'll be good. All of us. I promise." He turned to his cousin. "She means it, Luke. She's my sister. I know her."

"All right," said Luke sulkily.

Luke and David Michael's haircuts went fine after that. They even seemed reasonably satisfied with the results. David Michael made no references to owls.

Then came Berk and Andrew's turns. They protested as they climbed into the chairs, but behaved nicely after Mr. Gates promised them lollipops.

Pete and Patrick were last. Pete tried to kick Mr. Pratt in the shin, and Patrick cried the entire time. I sang seventeen verses of "Old MacDonald" to him, but it didn't help much, and Mr. Gates looked pained.

However, by the time we left, the barber shop and both barbers were still pretty much in one piece.

"We did it!" Mary Anne exclaimed as we were putting the littler boys in the wagon. "Somehow we did it!"

"I know! Now if I could just think of a wedding present to give Mom and Watson, this would be a perfect day."

"How about a toaster oven?" asked Mary Anne.

"Too expensive. Besides, Watson's got three."

"A tray," Luke suggested.

"We've got dozens."

"A picnic basket," said Berk.

"We've got one and Watson's got one."

"A fire engine," said Pete.

"A robot," said Patrick.

"Do I have to give them a present, too?" asked David Michael.

"It would be nice," I replied.

"Help me think of one, Kristy."

Oh, brother. *Two* presents?

# CHAPTER 11

*Wedding Countdown:*
*Friday — one day to go!*

Firday, June 26

Unfiar! Today it rained! all day!
I guess we baby sitters shouldnt
complain to much since this was the
first rainy day all weak. But still
it was a yucky day. wether wise.
The kids wore not to bad though.

Hey Kristy how come we have to
write in the diary this weak? Were
all sitting so we all know whats going
on right? I guess its just the rules
right? Anyway it cant hurt.

Anyway the morning went okay
but by the time lunch was over we
were running out of things to do
then I got this really fun idea ...

I have to admit, Claudia's idea was one of her better ones. As she mentioned, we used up all our regular ideas in the morning. The little kids watched *Sesame Street* and *Mister Rogers' Neighborhood*. The older kids played board games. Claudia set up some art activities, Dawn read aloud, and Mary Anne even plopped the babies in the playpen and helped Stacey's group bake cookies.

But by the time lunch was over, our ears were ringing with the sounds of:

"What can I do *now*, Kristy Dawn Stacey Mary Anne what's-your-name-again?"

"I don't *wanna* read another book."

"There's nothing *good* on TV."

"We *played* that already."

"Hey, let's give the babies a bath!" (That was Emma.)

"No!" cried Mary Anne.

Things were on the verge of getting out of hand. Ten of the fourteen children were crowded into our rec room. (The babies, Patrick, and Maura were asleep on a blanket in the living room.) Ashley was lying on the couch, moaning that her leg hurt and her head ached. Emma was tearing through the room after Katherine, who clearly did not enjoy being chased. Andrew and Grace were jumping up and down around Claudia, complaining that they didn't know what to do. In one corner was Karen with Berk and David Michael. She was talking to them earnestly and furtively (she kept glancing at Dawn), and from time to time I could hear the word *Martian*. Peter was using the couch as a trampoline. And Luke was lining up coffee cans on the floor. When I saw him bring a skateboard in from the garage and head for his obstacle course, I knew we were in trouble.

Stacey saw Luke at the same time, and talked him out of his activity.

At that point, I pulled the baby-sitters aside. "We've got to do something — *fast!*" I said. I looked outside. It was pouring.

"We need to separate them, first of all," said Dawn. "We should divide them into their groups and go off in different rooms. This is too much."

"Go off and do what, though? That's the problem," said Stacey. "They've done every-thing, already. They've been through every Kid-Kit, played every game, read every book, sung every song — "

"Okay, okay," said Dawn. "I still think we need to separate them."

"What would be fun," said Mary Anne thoughtfully, "would be a project for the whole group that the smaller groups could work on separately."

"You mean like putting on a show?" asked Claudia.

"Exactly," said Mary Anne.

"How about a talent show?" Dawn suggested. "Even the littlest kids could be in it."

"That would be fun," I said. "You know, we only have to occupy them until about four o'clock. Then we should start getting them dressed."

"Oh, yeah! I almost forgot," said Mary Anne.

The rehearsal dinner was to be held that night, and everyone, including the kids and us baby-sitters, had been invited. Actually, the Baby-sitters Club had been asked more to watch the kids than to be guests (although I would have gone anyway, of course), but it was still a good opportunity to get dressed in our very best clothes.

When Mom first told me about the special evening, I had to ask her what a rehearsal dinner was. It turns out that on the day before a wedding, the minister (or rabbi or priest) and the bride and groom and anyone who's going to be in the wedding get together to rehearse the ceremony, just as if it were a play. Afterward, the families, the people in the wedding, and a few special friends are invited to a big dinner, which is usually given by the groom's family.

In our case, what with the fourteen children and the crazy, last-minute preparations for the wedding, the schedule for the evening was wild. Finally, the adults had decided that things would go much more smoothly if my relatives didn't have to drive the kids all the way to their motels to dress for the dinner and then drive all the way back to Stoneybrook. So guess what? They asked the Baby-sitters Club to dress the children and have them ready for the evening when they were picked up at five o'clock.

After that, the members of the club (except for me) would go home, change quickly, and somehow get themselves to Watson's house. Meanwhile, the rest of us would go either to the rehearsal or to Watson's to help get ready for the dinner.

The children had shown up at my house that morning each carrying two bags. One bag was lunch, the other was clothes — a complete outfit. I had peeked in Maura's bag and seen a dress, a slip, a pair of tights, a change of underwear, party shoes, and barrettes. I hoped the other bags were as complete. Dressing fourteen kids for a fancy party had all the makings of a disaster.

But I couldn't worry about that then.

"You know," Claudia spoke up, grinning, "I just had a really funny idea. The rehearsal dinner made me think of it. Instead of putting on an ordinary show or play, how about putting on a wedding?"

"A wedding?" I exclaimed.

"Yeah. The kids can play all the different parts. Someone can be the bride, someone can be the groom. You know."

"You mean marry off a couple of the children?" said Stacey, laughing.

"Sure," replied Claudia. "The wedding is all these poor kids have heard about for the entire week. We might as well prepare them for the real thing. What do you think?"

We were all laughing by then.

"It's a great idea," I said.

"Do you still have those old clothes you used to play make-believe with?" asked Claudia.

"I can do better than that," I said. "Last year, out of the clear blue, Grandma — my other grandmother — sent us all these funny dress-up clothes. Some of the clothes would be perfect for our wedding. I'll go get them."

"We'll talk to the children," said Dawn.

By the time I returned to the rec room with

my load of clothes, the kids were sitting on the floor talking excitedly to Mary Anne, Stacey, Dawn, and Claudia.

"Well, we just chose the bride and groom," said Claudia.

Karen couldn't contain herself. "It's me! Me and David Michael!" she cried. "Because we're the same height."

The rest of the children volunteered for other parts in the ceremony. Luke was going to be the minister. Ashley reluctantly agreed to be the bride's mother (so she could sit down most of the time). Emma and Grace were to be the maids-of-honor, and Katherine wanted to be the flower girl. Berk decided to play the bride's father and give her away, Andrew and Peter decided to be ushers, and Patrick (who was awake and eager to participate) volunteered to be the ringbearer.

We divided into our groups and went off to rehearse the various parts and find costumes. Mary Anne watched the babies and helped with costumes. (Ashley had made a miraculous recovery from her various aches and pains.)

Half an hour later, we gathered in the rec room again to rehearse. The kids were dressed to the nines. David Michael had put on his best suit. (If he didn't wrinkle it, he could leave it on and wear it to the rehearsal dinner.) Mary Anne had found a top hat for him among the antique clothes. It was too big, but my brother liked it.

Karen, who loved to dress up, had put together the most amazing costume of all. She showed it off proudly.

"Here's my veil," she said, brushing aside a garish pink piece of netting, "and my lovely, lovely hat." (On top of the lovely, lovely hat was a lovely, lovely fake bird's nest with two fake bluebirds inside.) "And I put on my best bracelets. I guess my shoes are a little big" (they were a pair of Mom's) "but that's okay. Now, my dress is the most beautiful part of all. See the jewels?"

The dress was wilder than the veil. For starters, it wasn't white; it was bright blue, with shimmery sequins sewn all over it. The waistline fell around Karen's knees.

"That's a *wedding* dress?" cried Ashley. "Wedding dresses are supposed to be white. Or maybe they could be yellow or something, but not *that!*"

Karen looked crushed. "Kristy?" she asked in a small voice.

"Well, technically," I said, "a wedding dress can be any color."

Karen stuck her tongue out at Ashley. *"See?"*

*"See?"* Ashley mimicked her.

"Okay, okay, you guys," said Claudia. "Let's not spoil the wedding."

"But I'm her mother," Ashley protested. "Aren't mothers supposed to complain?"

I giggled. "Maybe," I replied, "but let's just go on, okay?"

The kids ran through their parts. When they knew them pretty well, they looked at us expectantly.

"Let me get the camera!" I said suddenly. "I'll be the wedding photographer." I found Mom's Polaroid, hoping she wouldn't mind if I borrowed it. "Into the living room, you guys. We'll have the wedding in there, if you promise to be careful."

"Oh, we will! We will!" the kids chorused.

"All right, then. Places, everyone."

Luke stood importantly in front of the fireplace. David Michael and Patrick (the ringbearer) were next to him.

Andrew and Peter (the ushers) led Ashley and the baby-sitters with the three little children to seats on the couches and armchairs. Then they joined Luke, David Michael, and Patrick at the front of the room.

"Okay, bridesmaids," I whispered to Emma

and Grace, who were peeping into the living room.

The girls walked slowly through the room, Grace tripping over the hem of her long dress with every step.

They positioned themselves on the other side of Luke.

Katherine came next, wearing what looked like a ballerina's tutu, and tossing confetti out of an old Easter basket. Karen, the beautiful bride, followed with Berk at her side.

She joined David Michael, they turned to face Luke, and Berk sat down next to Ashley.

Click, click. Click, click. I was trying to record every important moment.

"Ladies and gentlemen," said Luke solemnly, beginning a speech he had made up, and which seemed to change every time he recited it, "we are gathered here today to join these two guys in . . . in. . . ." He looked helplessly at Stacey. "What did you say it was called?"

"Holy matrimony," Stacey whispered.

"In . . . in holy moly." (The baby-sitters managed not to laugh.) "Weddings are very important," Luke continued. "You have to know what you're getting into. If you think you're ready, then you can take the oath. Are you ready?"

"We're ready," said Karen and David Michael.

"Okay, then. Karen, do you promise to love your husband and help him out and not hog the television?"

"I guess so," said Karen.

"Okay. And David Michael, do you promise to love your wife and help her out and show her how to ride a two-wheeler?"

"I guess."

"Okay. By the way, are you two going to have any kids?"

"Yes," said Karen.

"No," said David Michael.

"Well, if you do, be nice to them, all right?"

"Yeah," spoke up Berk. "Don't give them any bedtimes."

"And don't yell at them when they forget to feed the dog," added Luke.

"And once in a while," said Emma, "let them go into a toy store and when they say, 'Can I have this?' you say, 'Yes,' even if it costs forty dollars."

"All right," said the bride and groom.

"Great." Luke nodded to Patrick.

Patrick handed David Michael a ring, and my brother slipped it on Karen's finger.

"You may now kiss the bride!" Luke announced triumphantly.

*"What?!"* shrieked David Michael, and his hat fell down over his eyes. "You never said *that* before!"

"Ew, ew!" cried Karen.

My last photo of the wedding showed Karen and David Michael running, horror-stricken, from the living room.

It was time to get ready for the (real) rehearsal dinner.

# CHAPTER 12

*Wedding Countdown:*
*Friday evening — half a day to go*

As soon as we got Karen and David Michael calmed down, it was time to begin dressing the children for the dinner at Watson's. I handed the bags containing the clothing to the baby-sitters, and they went off to various parts of the house with their groups. I took Grace, Katherine, and Andrew (who were not modest) into the playroom to change.

My first clue that anything was wrong was when I opened Andrew's bag and pulled out a yellow dress.

"Oops," I said. "Wrong bag. Katherine, this must be yours. Or yours, Grace."

"Not mine," said Katherine.

"Not mine," said Grace.

I checked the bag again. Sure enough, it was labeled ANDREW.

"Hmm," I said.

"Hey, Kristy!" Mary Anne called from the kitchen. "Come here."

"You guys stay right there," I told the yellow group. "What is it, Mary Anne?"

"Look at this," she said as I entered the kitchen. She held up a bow tie and a pair of gray flannel trousers. "I found these in Beth's bag. And this slip in Tony's bag," she added, showing me a lacy, white undergarment. "It's got to be Ashley's. It's too big for any of the other girls."

Just as Claudia, sounding exasperated, called to me from the living room, Stacey marched into the kitchen, pushing Emma along in front of her. "Okay, Emma Meiner, tell your cousin what you told me."

Emma looked as if she couldn't decide whether to giggle or cry.

"Emma . . ." Stacey said, nudging her.

"I switched the clothes," Emma whispered.

*"What?"* I squawked.

"I switched the clothes," she repeated, more loudly. "Not all of them. Just one or two things from each bag. I did it while you were getting lunch."

"Emma!" I shouted. I was angry. I don't usually get angry when I'm baby-sitting, but Emma had made me *really* angry. The Baby-sitters Club had been anxious to prove that it could be responsible for a large group of children, and it had done a good job right up until now — four o'clock on Friday afternoon. I couldn't believe Emma was going to make us look bad in the final hour of our biggest job ever.

"Emma . . ." I said again, trying to control my temper.

"Yes?" she answered, and a tear slipped down her cheek.

"Emma, what you did was really naughty. It's four o'clock. There's only one hour until our parents are going to come get us for the rehearsal dinner. They expect us — *all* of us — to be dressed and ready then. Thanks to you, we might not be ready after all. Now, while we sort out the clothes, I want you to sit by yourself in the den and think about what you did."

I led her into our den and sat her on the couch. "Sit there and don't move. Don't touch anything. Just sit and think." I closed the door.

Then I gathered all the baby-sitters, all the children (except Emma), and all the bags of clothing in the living room. It took a half an hour, but finally we were pretty sure we had the right clothes in the right bags. Some of the clothes were labeled with nametags, the older children recognized their clothes and most of the things belonging to their little brothers and sisters, and my friends and I used common sense to figure out what was left over.

At four-thirty we divided up again, and I let Emma out of the den.

"I'm sorry, Kristy," she said, and I felt sort of mean. I could tell she'd been crying.

"And I'm sorry I got mad. But promise me you won't do anything else naughty today. Or tomorrow," I added, thinking of what could happen while the wedding was in progress. "We all have to be on our best behavior."

"I promise," said Emma in a small voice.

"Okay," I replied. I gave her a hug. Then I sent her off with Stacey.

Half an hour later, fourteen very dressy children were milling around our living room. Their parents had not shown up yet.

"Hey, how about a picture?" I asked. There were two shots left on the roll of film in the Polaroid.

"Yes! Yes!" cried the kids.

Claudia, the artistic one, began to pose them. "You big kids sit on the couch. . . . No, not on the *back* of the couch, Berk. Just *on* the couch, like a regular person. Okay, good. And you shorter kids sit on the floor in front of them. Katherine, hold your little brother, okay? No, *hold* him. He's sliding over. Grace, give Beth a hand. She's escaping. Put her in your lap, okay?"

Claudia turned to me. "Hurry, Kristy! Before they move!"

I snapped the picture. When the film was developed, we saw that Tony was slumped over so you couldn't see his face, Beth was pulling Grace's hair, two kids had their eyes closed, and Berk was poking David Michael in the side.

"Let's try it again," I said. "We have one more picture left. Now this time, open your eyes, look at the camera, smile, and don't poke anybody!"

Click!

The second picture was perfect.

And the kids were still posed at the couch when the adults walked in.

There was much oohing and aahing.

"Aren't they adorable?"

"Oh, who's this handsome crowd?!"

"Wouldn't this make a cute Christmas card?"

"Isn't Patrick wearing somebody else's tie?"

"What's Beth doing wearing tights?"

The members of the Baby-sitters Club glanced at each other, then at Emma. Nobody said a word. We weren't about to tell.

Luckily, there wasn't time to worry about the clothes. The kids looked gorgeous, anyway. So the aunts and uncles and the Fieldings drove their kids, plus Karen and Andrew, back to Watson's. The other members of the Baby-sitters Club left to get dressed.

When they were gone, I turned to Mom. "Gosh, the house feels *empty*," I said. "I'm really going to miss those kids."

"We won't," spoke up Sam and Charlie. They had been pretty scarce all week. That evening, they had managed not to come home until precisely five minutes after everyone had left.

"I might miss them," said David Michael, "and I might not." He ran upstairs to his room.

"He won't miss sharing," I informed my mother, "but he'll miss having kids his own age around."

"Maybe," said Mom thoughtfully, "he and Karen will get along better than I think."

I beamed with pleasure, but as I passed Sam on my way into the kitchen, I heard him mutter, "Don't lay any bets on it."

I won't bother you with the details of the rehearsal itself. All you need to know is that it went reasonably well, considering we were rehearsing an outdoor wedding in the all-purpose room of a church, and that Karen, upon hearing that the florist shop was not going to be able to provide her with yellow rose petals and that she'd have to make do with white ones instead, turned pale and widened her eyes until I thought they'd spring out of their sockets.

"What's wrong?" her father asked, alarmed.

"*White* petals," moaned Karen. "They mean white magic. Morbidda Destiny will be right next door with her black magic. The two magics will crash into each other — BA-ROOM — and then. . . ." Karen made a slashing motion across her throat.

David Michael screamed.

"What?" said the confused minister.

"Nothing, nothing," Watson replied hurriedly. "Karen, not another word about that nonsense. Not *one*."

But Karen didn't say anything, and I knew that meant she wasn't agreeing to keep her mouth shut.

Everyone but me forgot about Karen and the magics.

The dinner at Watson's was really fun. All us baby-sitters were as dressed up as if we were going to an important school dance. Claudia had helped me choose a new dress the week before. It was a gigantic white sweater with silver designs woven into it. It was a very un-Kristy-type dress — and I felt glamorous.

During the dinner, which was eaten at two long tables in Watson's dining room, the babysitters had to help the kids and keep them quiet. But afterward, we were more like guests. I showed my friends the room that I had recently decided I'd like for my bedroom.

"It's . . . it's *big*," said Dawn, awed.

"Think of the slumber parties we can have here," added Stacey.

"Think what you can do with the room," said Claudia. "A mural on the wall. . . . Maybe you'll get a canopy bed or something."

"Yeah," I said slowly. "More important, it doesn't look into Morbidda Destiny's house, after all. It doesn't look into yours, either, Mary Anne, but the backyard is better than Mrs. Porter's."

"I guess," answered Mary Anne sadly.

The highlight of the evening came as the dinner was drawing to an end. Watson and Mom took the members of the Baby-sitters Club aside and handed us each an envelope containing a check for one hundred and thirty dollars.

"That's one hundred and twenty for a job *very* well done," Mom told us.

"And a ten-dollar bonus," added Watson.

I gawked at my friends. We were rich!

After we got through thanking Mom and Watson and saying good-bye to everyone, it was time to go home. The next day was . . . the wedding!

(And I still had no idea what to give Mom and Watson.)

# CHAPTER 13

*Wedding Countdown:*
*Saturday — Zero Hour*

"Ee-iiii!"

It was the Big Day, the day of the wedding.

I woke up with a start and leaped out of bed without really knowing why. Then I remembered. I had to see what the weather was like. The day before had been rainy. If it was still rainy, then (horror of horrors) the wedding would have to be held indoors. The guests would be jammed into Watson's living room like sardines in a can.

I stood at the window and picked up the corner of the shade, but I couldn't bear to pull it back.

If it was raining, Mom would be in one of her moods.

I gathered my courage and lifted the shade.

I was greeted by a clear, blue sky.

"Oh, thank you, thank you, thank you!" I exclaimed. "Now if I could just get an idea for a wedding present."

I ran downstairs thinking, Coffee cups? No. Cheese server? No. Paperweight? No. Pitcher? No. . . .

The wedding wasn't until two o'clock in the afternoon, but the morning went by in a flash. There was still a lot to do. Nannie came over to help us out. She gave Mom a hand packing for the honeymoon. Then she and Mom rode to the beauty salon in the Pink Clinker to get their hair done. When they came back, Nannie made us all eat something.

"I'd hate for one of you to faint during the ceremony," she said.

"But I'm too nervous to eat," Mom replied.

"Just a little something," Nannie insisted, and suddenly she sounded very much like the mother, and Mom like the daughter.

After we'd eaten enough to please Nannie, it was time to get dressed. I went to my room, closed the door, and, with a feeling of awe, took my bridesmaid gown out of the closet. It had been hanging there in a plastic dry cleaner's bag since the day before.

I was about to put it on when something

occurred to me. I ran to my window. "Hey, Mary Anne!" I shouted. I hoped she was in her room. "Mary Anne!"

Mary Anne's head appeared in her window.

"Come over!" I called. "You want to help me get dressed?"

"Sure!"

Mary Anne was in my room in a flash. She helped me remove the dress from the bag. Then she zipped me into it.

The dress fit perfectly. Nannie had done a terrific job.

"Oh, Kristy," whispered Mary Anne, "you look beautiful!"

"Thanks," I replied. "I feel kind of beautiful."

I put on my white knee-high stockings and my new shoes with the heels.

"What if I *trip?*" I cried, the awful thought slamming into my mind like a truck.

"You won't," Mary Anne assured me.

My bouquet and the flowers for my hair had been delivered to Watson's, so I was as dressed as I could get for the time being. When Mom and Nannie and my brothers were dressed, too (we looked so elegant!), Nannie whisked us over to Watson's.

"See you at the wedding!" I called to Mary Anne from the window of the Pink Clinker.

At the Brewers' house, Mom and Watson were not allowed to see each other (it was supposed to be bad luck or something), so Mom and Karen and I were taken into a spare bedroom, where Nannie put the finishing touches on us.

Karen was overexcited. She jumped up and down and danced around the room. "Oh, I'm the little flower girl," she sang. "The flower girl, the flower girl. And here are my white magic petals — "

"Karen, sweetie," said Mom patiently, "sit down for a minute. You're going to wear yourself out."

"Mom! Oh, no!" I cried suddenly.

"What is it, Kristy?" Mom asked, alarmed.

"It's a little late for this, but do you have something old, something new, something borrowed, and something blue?"

"Believe it or not, I do," said Mom. "My earrings are antiques, my dress is new, I borrowed Nannie's pearl necklace, and, well, some of my underwear is blue — pale blue."

Karen began to giggle.

"That's a relief," I said.

Nannie left the room for a moment, and Andrew wandered in. His shoes were untied, his shirt was unbuttoned, his hair was a mess, and he was trailing his necktie along the floor.

"Andrew!" exclaimed my mother. "You should be ready by now, honey."

"Everybody's busy," Andrew wailed, "and I need help."

"I'll help you," I said. I put Andrew together and sent him out into the hall, where I caught sight of the Fieldings. "Andrew, you're going to sit with your friends. There are Katherine and Patrick. Stay with them, okay?"

Just as Andrew was running off, Nannie returned. "It's time!" she said excitedly.

Mom and Nannie hugged each other.

I ran to the window and peeped outside. The street in front of Watson's house was lined with cars. "Everybody's here already?" I squeaked.

"They're seated and waiting," replied Nannie.

Yikes!

"Now are you two *sure* you know what to do?" Mom asked Karen and me for the eighty-zillionth time.

"Yes," said Karen.

"Positive," I said.

"All right. Let's go."

Nannie led us through Watson's house to the door to the patio. There we were met by Sam and Charlie, looking handsome and solemn and somehow not much like my big brothers.

Sam escorted Nannie down the aisle between the folding chairs, and seated her in the front row. The guests watched, murmuring approvingly. Then he joined Watson, who was standing with David Michael (the ringbearer) and the minister in front of the guests.

I drew in my breath. I hadn't really had a good look at the yard until then, and I saw that it was beautiful. The minister and my brothers were separated from the guests by garlands of flowers strung between poles. Behind the minister was a sort of arbor, covered with more flowers. It all would have been perfect if not for the sight of Morbidda Destiny's house beyond.

"Okay, Kristy. You're next, honey," said Mom.

There was a piano player on the patio, and he struck up the wedding march. I stood still for a moment, collecting myself. Then, holding my bouquet firmly in front of me, I walked slowly up the aisle. I was aware that everyone had turned around to look at me. I tried to smile, especially when I spotted Mary Anne and Claudia, but my mouth trembled as if I were going to cry.

The aisle looked a mile long, but at last I reached the garlands of flowers. I stepped through them and stood next to the minister, on the other side of him from my brothers and Watson. When I was able to focus on the people in front of me, I saw Karen walking jauntily up that long aisle in front of my mother, who was escorted by Charlie. Karen was strewing her rose petals and grinning broadly. No stage fright for her.

When Mom walked by Nannie, Nannie burst into tears.

In all honesty, I have to say that the next part of the wedding, the vows and stuff, got kind of boring. I stopped paying attention and looked out at the guests. Mary Anne smiled at me. So did Dawn. Jamie Newton waved and called out, "Hi-hi!" which made several people laugh.

Just as the minister was saying, "You may kiss the bride," I noticed Stacey signaling frantically. She was pointing to me. . . . No, not to me, to Karen. I looked down. Karen had turned around and was staring at something behind us. From the look on her face, I thought for sure Dracula was back there.

Then Karen let out an ear-piercing shriek. Luckily, she let it loose just when Mom and Watson were finishing their kiss (a very big smooch, I might add), and people were beginning to rise from their seats with congratulations.

The ceremony was over.

I dared to turn around.

Morbidda Destiny was standing behind me in full black dress, with her snapping eyes and her frazzly, witchy hair.

"The magics!" Karen wailed. "The magics are going to crash!"

Morbidda Destiny looked at Karen, puzzled. Then she turned to me. "I brought the bride and groom something," she said, holding out a box.

"Don't take it!" Karen cried. "It's a wedding spell! It's a — "

A hand was clapped over Karen's mouth. Watson had broken away from the celebrating.

"Why, thank you, Mrs. Porter," he said, accepting the box with one hand, while keeping his other hand over Karen's mouth. "That's very nice of you. Won't you join the guests for some refreshm— Ow!"

Karen had tried to bite her father's hand. *"Daddy — "*

I pulled Karen away. Watson regained his composure, and Mrs. Porter did stay at the party for a while. (Karen ran in the house and wouldn't come out until she was gone.)

Later, the caterer wheeled out the wedding cake. The guests gathered around to watch Mom and Watson cut the first slice. They did it together, both pressing down on the cake-cutter. Then they each took a bite of cake, their wrists intertwined. I could see their wedding rings shining in the sunlight.

They're joined, I thought. They're part of each other, and our families have come together to be part of each other, too.

I felt tears spring to my eyes.

And at that moment, I knew what to give Mom and my stepfather.

# CHAPTER 14

"Good-bye! Good-bye!"

One after another, our relatives' station wagons pulled away from Watson's house. The wedding was over, the guests were gone, and now our family was leaving, too.

"See you, Luke! 'Bye, Emma! Behave yourself. Bye-bye, Beth!"

The Meiners were gone.

"Take care of your leg, Ashley! 'Bye, Peter! 'Bye, Grace!"

"May the force be with you!" (That was David Michael saying good-bye to Berk.)

The Millers were gone.

A friend of Watson's pulled up, picked up Karen and Andrew to take them to their mother's, and then *they* were gone.

Last to leave were Mom and Watson. They were going to spend their honeymoon at a little inn in Vermont. My brothers and I would be on our own for a week!

Before Mom got in the car, she ran through a list of last-minute instructions.

"Don't forget to walk Louie before you go to bed. And don't forget to change his water. And lock up the house if you're all going to be out. Charlie, you're in charge. David Michael, remember your vitamins."

"Aw, *Mom*."

"And Sam — "

"Mom, Mom, we know *every*thing," I said. "Trust us. We won't leave the burners on — "

"Oh, I hadn't even *thought* of that," exclaimed Mom.

" — and we'll run the dishwasher, and we know where the emergency money is."

"And I'll be on call," spoke up Nannie, who was standing behind us. Nannie was going to drop my brothers and me off at our house, and then go home. She looked tired.

"Honey, let's go," said Watson.

"Oh . . . all right." Mom tried to hug all of us at once.

I kissed Watson on the cheek and he told me I'd been a beautiful bridesmaid.

Two minutes later, Mom and Watson were gone, too. Watson honked the horn all the way down the street.

When Nannie dropped Charlie, Sam, David

Michael, and me off, we waved to her as the Pink Clinker hummed down the street. Then we went inside, and all four of us collapsed on the floor in the living room. Louie joined us, lolling on his back.

Just when I thought every last one of my brothers was asleep, the silence was interrupted by a snort of laughter from Charlie. Then he said in a deep voice, "All right, you guys. You heard Mom. I'm in charge. These are the house rules."

I raised my eyebrows. Leave it to Charlie to let a little responsibility go to his head.

"Dinner every night will be pizza. Everyone must go to bed an hour later than usual. Sam, no eating in the kitchen; food is permitted only in front of the TV set *while it's on*. Kristy, you must, I repeat *must*, spend three hours a day talking on the phone. David Michael, go through the *TV Guide* and make sure you don't miss a single cartoon show."

"Do I still have to take my vitamins?" he asked, inspired.

"Yes," replied Charlie. "Don't press your luck."

The four of us were laughing hysterically. It was a good thing, because I'd been just about ready to leak a few tears over the wedding, and Mom's being gone and all.

Instead, when we recovered from Charlie's rules, I went to my room and began working on my idea for the present. Eventually I'd need Claudia's help, but I might as well get my thoughts together before I talked to her. I looked through our encyclopedia for information on family trees. I doodled a bit. I hoped I would have the present ready by the time my mother and stepfather came back.

That night, before David Michael went to bed, he stuck his head in my room and said, "Hey, Kristy, I know what to give Mom and Watson."

"What?" I asked.

"Goldfish," he replied.

And that's exactly what he did give them.

The next day, I talked to Claudia about my idea. I went over to her house so we could look at her art supplies.

"See? It'll show both families," I said, "and how they became one. But I need help with the design. And I need you to draw a bow and show me how to make those little flowers you drew on that art project for Mr. Fineman last year."

"Or maybe you should use a real bow," suggested Claudia.

"Oh, that's an idea! And maybe the background could be a really pretty piece of wall-paper or something."

Claudia and I bent busily over our work.

We were interrupted later by the sound of the doorbell. That was followed by the sound of feet — lots of them — running up the stairs. Stacey, Dawn, and Mary Anne appeared in the doorway to Claudia's room.

"Hi, you guys!" said Dawn. "We were looking for you."

"Look what I've got," said Stacey. "Pictures." She held out a fat envelope. "They're from the wedding. Mom and I took them to that one-hour developing place downtown. It was open this morning."

"Ooh!" I shrieked. "Let's see."

Claudia and I abandoned our project. The five of us plunked down on the floor, and my friends peered over my shoulders as I opened the envelope.

"There you are, getting ready to walk up the aisle," said Stacey. "And there you are, walking up the aisle."

"Look at the expression on my face!" I cried.

"You look so nervous!" said Mary Anne.

"No, she looks like she's going to cry!" exclaimed Dawn.

"Both, I think," I said. "Gosh, the dress looks pretty, though, doesn't it?"

"Beautiful."

"Perfect."

"Where is it now?"

"What are you going to do with it?"

We were all talking at once.

"It's in my closet in a plastic bag," I told them. "I don't know what I'm going to do with it. I'll probably outgrow it pretty soon."

"Oh, don't!" wailed Mary Anne. "If *you* start growing, then *I'll* be the class shrimp."

"Hey, there's Mom and Watson kissing!" I exclaimed. "Stacey, I can't believe you took a picture of them doing *that!*"

Stacey grinned slyly. "I thought you'd want the moment captured forever."

I poked her.

"There's Karen and you and Watson and Morbidda Destiny," said Mary Anne softly. She shuddered.

"It's hard to believe Mor— Mrs. Porter is going to be my neighbor soon," I whispered. I quickly stuck the photo on the bottom of the pile. "Here are Mom and Watson cutting the cake," I said, looking at the next picture. "That's a great photo, Stacey. Hey, you guys, that's what gave me the idea for a wedding present for Mom and Watson."

"What is?" asked Stacey.

"Mom and Watson, when they linked their wrists like that and stuff. Like in the picture. I thought of how their coming together brought our families together to make another different family. And then I thought I could make them a sort of family tree to show the new family. Claudia's helping me. See what we're going to do?"

I showed them what Claudia and I were working on. "Up at the top," I explained, "are Karen and Andrew. Then those lines show that they're Watson's children. In the middle, Mom and Watson are joined by a heart. And the lines under Mom's name show that my brothers and I are her children. And that's the new family."

"That's really something," said Mary Anne.

"Yeah," agreed Dawn. "I think it will mean a lot to your mom."

"I wonder if I can get it framed before the honeymoon is over," I said.

"I bet my mother and I could go with you to the frame store this week, if you wanted help," said Stacey.

"Really? Thanks!"

The members of the Baby-sitters Club looked

at my new family tree. Mom and Watson, Karen and Andrew, Charlie and Sam and David Michael and me. Two families coming together to make a new family. That's what the wedding had been all about.

# About the Author

ANN M. MARTIN did *a lot* of baby-sitting when she was growing up in Princeton, New Jersey. Now her favorite baby-sitting charge is her cat, Mouse, who lives with her in her Manhattan apartment.

Ann Martin's Apple Paperbacks are *Bummer Summer, Inside Out, Stage Fright, Me and Katie (the Pest)*, and all the other books in the Baby-sitters Club series.

She is a former editor of books for children, and was graduated from Smith College. She likes ice cream, the beach, and *I Love Lucy*; and she hates to cook.

# America's Favorite Series

**THE BABY-SITTERS CLUB®**

*Collect Them All!*

### by Ann M. Martin

The seven girls at Stoneybrook Middle School get into
all kinds of adventures...with school, boys, and, of course, baby-sitting!

# APPLE® *Classics*

## Exciting adventures that kids everywhere have loved for a long time...so will you!